'I've neveu before.'

Her lips curved upwards, slowly, tentatively. 'That's a good thing?'

'You bet,' he said, using every ounce of self-control to lower his head slowly and graze her lips with his, when in fact he wanted to devour her.

'You kiss real good for a hermit,' she murmured.

'This is it. Last chance to back out, change the ground rules, come to your senses, whatever,' he said, lifting her hair off the nape of her neck and nibbling his way downwards towards her collarbone.

'I'll take the whatever.'

His head lifted, their gazes locked, and time stood still with the heady anticipation of what they were about to do.

Dear Reader

Writing is my passion. I love nothing better than to sit at my keyboard, concoct characters and let their stories flow.

In short, writing is my dream job—something Bo Bradford, the ultra-sexy hero in TWO-WEEK MISTRESS, can identify with. Bo is so caught up in his craft as a bestselling children's author that he can't see what's right in front of him, namely one gorgeous illustrator: Tahnee Lewis.

A self-proclaimed recluse, Bo lives in a fantasy world peppered with his cute critters for company. While I can understand Bo's need to live, eat and breathe with his characters, I'm happy to say I have a life away from my keyboard! Bo doesn't, but all that's about to change...

Tahnee Lewis is more than a match for the hermit author, and soon has him getting creative in a variety of ways, most of which don't involve words...

I hope you enjoy an insight into an author's mind. (Bo's, not mine. Really!)

Happy reading

Nicola

www.nicolamarsh.com

TWO-WEEK MISTRESS

BY
NICOLA MARSH

DID YOU PURCHASE THIS BOOK WITHOUT A COVER?

If you did, you should be aware it is **stolen property** as it was reported *unsold and destroyed* by a retailer. Neither the author nor the publisher has received any payment for this book.

All the characters in this book have no existence outside the imagination of the author, and have no relation whatsoever to anyone bearing the same name or names. They are not even distantly inspired by any individual known or unknown to the author, and all the incidents are pure invention.

All Rights Reserved including the right of reproduction in whole or in part in any form. This edition is published by arrangement with Harlequin Enterprises II B.V. The text of this publication or any part thereof may not be reproduced or transmitted in any form or by any means, electronic or mechanical, including photocopying, recording, storage in an information retrieval system, or otherwise, without the written permission of the publisher.

This book is sold subject to the condition that it shall not, by way of trade or otherwise, be lent, resold, hired out or otherwise circulated without the prior consent of the publisher in any form of binding or cover other than that in which it is published and without a similar condition including this condition being imposed on the subsequent purchaser.

MILLS & BOON and MILLS & BOON with the Rose Device are registered trademarks of the publisher.

First published in Great Britain 2007
Harlequin Mills & Boon Limited,
Eton House, 18-24 Paradise Road, Richmond, Surrey TW9 1SR

© Nicola Marsh 2007

ISBN-13: 978 0 263 85385 8
ISBN-10:   0 263 85385 3

Set in Times Roman 10½ on 12¾ pt
171-0307-48253

Printed and bound in Spain
by Litografia Rosés, S.A., Barcelona

TWO-WEEK MISTRESS

To the many friends I've made through my writing.
This one's for all of you.

CHAPTER ONE

Wally the Wombat waddled out into the sunshine and blinked. This wasn't a good day. His friend Mandy the Mole had upped and left him after getting married. No, this wouldn't do at all. He had to find a new friend to help him dig all day. Fast.
Bo Bradford's blog, Sunday.

'HOW CUTE is that?'

Tahnee Lewis looked up from the computer screen and rolled her eyes at her best friend, Nina. 'You think that's cute? Wait till you see the pictures I come up with to dazzle the elusive Bo Bradford.'

Nina smiled and slid into the ergonomic chair next to her. 'I have no doubt you'll dazzle this guy and become world famous and probably never speak to me ever again. But what I want to know is—does he usually use Wally as a substitute for himself? It's cute, but kind of sad, too.'

Tahnee shrugged, her gaze drawn back to the screen with its colourful graphics and quirky little animal drawings, which, to her critical and purely objective eye, weren't a patch on what she could produce, of course.

'I have no idea. That's why I did an Internet search and this blog is all I can come up with. His website is limited to a backlist of books and he doesn't have a bio.'

'Don't most authors have bios on their websites?'

'Uh-huh, and this makes the elusive Mr Bradford all the more intriguing.'

When starting out in the publishing business, Tahnee would've given her best charcoals to work for a guy like Bo Bradford: Australia's number one children's author, whose every book was a certifiable winner. His reputation hadn't dimmed in the last four years, and, though she could hold her own as a top illustrator, she knew working with him would guarantee her steady work for life.

'You're actually going to live with this guy for two weeks? And you know nothing about him?'

A small frown creased Nina's brow, the same frown she wore when Marian, her adorable daughter, or Callum, her son, got into mischief.

'Relax. My publisher put me in touch with his agent, who organised the whole thing. Bo's on the up and up; I'll be living in a semi-detached flat attached to his place and this arrangement is going to be a win-win for both of us. He needs a new illustrator, I need a new job. And if all goes well, he'll hire me on a permanent basis.'

And this was one job she really needed.

She was so close to achieving her lifelong dream that not even having her publisher go under could deter her now. But she had to admit: she needed the money this job would bring.

Nina's frown didn't disappear. 'Yeah, but what's with having you live in? The guy could be some sort of weirdo.'

The same thought had crossed her mind, but the publishing world was small and she'd asked a few discreet questions and was more than satisfied the mysterious Bo Bradford was on the level.

'He writes children's books. Do you see Wally the wombat having some kind of strange S and M fetish?'

Nina's concerned gaze flicked to the PC screen and her frown vanished. 'Good point. I guess a guy who spends his days creating cute little critters like Wally can't be all bad.'

'Exactly. Now, you want to help me pack or what?'

'Like it's going to take you long to pack ten pairs of jeans, your oldest denim jacket and the few tops you throw on under it.'

Tahnee stood and placed a hand on her hip, thrusting out a leg clad in her favourite dark denim. 'Are you trying to tell me something about my wardrobe?'

Nina grinned. 'Only the same thing I've been trying to tell you since high school.'

'What? That not all men are attracted to denim?' She waggled her finger under Nina's nose. 'I've got news for you. The guys I date like it just fine.'

'Riiiight. And your last date was?'

Okay, so her know-it-all, disgustingly happily married friend had a point. It had been a while—ten months to be exact.

Not that she was counting or anything.

'All I'm trying to say is you don't know anything about this guy, so it mightn't hurt to pack a few extras.'

Nina's blue eyes glazed over in that dreamy, romantic haze she usually reserved for talking about her husband, Karl, the local mechanic who had taken one look at her best friend and turned into a marshmallow. 'Who knows? He might expect you to dress up for dinner.'

Tahnee laughed and shook her head.

'What century are you living in? Jeez, you've turned into a total sap since you got married.'

'Nothing wrong with wanting my friend to be happy,' Nina said, a goofy grin on her face to match the gleam in her eyes.

'You're so right. I'll make sure all the single men in Stockton know you're on the warpath.'

Nina chuckled. 'You always have to have the last word.'

'Too right. Now, I have a few hundred pairs of jeans that need folding, so want to help?'

Nina threw a cushion at her and she ducked, knowing she'd miss this, even for a fortnight.

Discovering her sisters Carissa and Kristen six years earlier had been a spin out. They'd been separated as youngsters following the death of their parents and getting to know her real family had been a blast. But it was Nina's life-long friendship that had sustained her in the early years of coming to Stockton and living with a foster family. Still did.

Since she'd met Nina at primary school, they'd been virtually inseparable. Until big, bad Karl came on the scene, that is, and her best friend turned into a soppy romantic, though thankfully she still saw a lot of Nina and her adorable kids.

Family and friends were important to her, security even more so, but, if she had to live with an eccentric stranger for two weeks in order to secure her career, then so be it.

Yeah, she could do this.

Two weeks in Sydney would be a breeze and winning over the reclusive Bo Bradford would be her number-one priority.

If he turned out to be a psycho, she'd just stab him with her sharpest pencil.

Bo Bradford hated technology.

He hated wasting precious hours on updating his blog every day in the name of promotion.

He hated telephones, which broke his concentration, and faxes, which interrupted his thought processes.

And he especially hated the damn intercom, which signalled the arrival of his replacement illustrator.

Clasping his fingers and stretching forwards, he pushed away from his desk and headed for the elaborate intercom system he'd had installed five years earlier when protecting his privacy became all important.

Stabbing at the talk button, he said, 'Yes?'

'Tahnee Lewis here, reporting for duty.'

Bo reared back from the intercom as if the woman had stuck her finger through it and poked him in the eye.

She had a sense of humour? Great.

He didn't need a comedienne, he needed a gun illustrator, and, though she'd come highly recommended, he believed in the old motto 'seeing is believing.' Past work didn't count; he needed to see what she could achieve on his books.

Hitting the talk button again, he said, 'Drive through. I'll meet you round the back.'

'Round the back, huh? Right-o.'

Static crackled for several seconds and he realised he hadn't moved, something in the woman's voice captivating his attention.

She sounded young. Too young.

He needed an expert, not someone to baby-sit, and the faster he filled Moira's position, the better.

She also had a tone, a challenging tone that he didn't like. She'd made it sound like he'd told her to come in the servants' entrance, when in fact he didn't have servants and used the back entrance all the time because it led into the kitchen and family room, the most welcoming and lived-in parts of the house.

Damn it, he shouldn't make snap judgements, but ever since Moira had upped and left him in the lurch he'd been floundering—okay, so the quiet, mousy woman who had had the longest engagement in history had warned him she'd be out of here once the wedding ring was slipped on her finger.

But he had a deadline to meet and a position to fill and he'd placed a lot of faith in Tahnee Lewis. She had better be able to come up with the goods.

A funny knock reminiscent of the beat of an old eighties' tune came from the kitchen door and he quickly saved the word document he'd been working on and headed out the back.

He was big on first impressions, always had been; the minute he opened the door, he knew he was in trouble.

'Bo Bradford? I'm Tahnee Lewis, pleased to meet you.'

Bo shook her hand automatically, trying not to stare at the tall, stunning blonde standing on his doorstep, and failing miserably.

He'd been expecting a professionally dressed woman with a hopeful look on her face.

What he got was a denim-clad-student type with a challenge in her deep blue eyes and a cheeky quirk to her full lips.

This woman didn't look like the subservient type willing to take orders from a grumpy author subject to creative whims.

With the face of a naughty devil and the body of an angel, she looked like one thing to him.

Trouble.

'Did I catch you at a bad time?'

Bo silently cursed his ineptitude, dropped her hand quickly and stepped aside. 'No, come in. I was just in the middle of a scene and I tend to get a bit distracted.'

'I know exactly what you mean. I do the same thing myself. Just the other day, I was so into a sketch that the toaster had a tussle with a piece of bread resulting in smoke filling the kitchen, and I didn't even notice.'

She smiled and his heart sank.

Her face lit up with the type of million-dollar smile that could sell toothpaste to dentists. Combine that with the sparkling blue eyes, lush mouth and long blond hair cut into layers which framed her heart-shaped face, and Bo knew she might prove to be more of a distraction than any scene.

'Do you need a hand with any more bags?'

He pointed to a small wheelie suitcase and a backpack, expecting another bag or ten in the car. The women he'd dated in the past had always needed at least five bags or cases of various sizes to go anywhere for more than a week. Yet another reason why he preferred living and travelling on his own.

'No, this is it.'

He tried to mask his shock, but must've failed by the twitching corners of her mouth.

That mouth… His gaze flickered past it, desperately trying to stay focused on her eyes. However, the harder he fought, the more tempting it became till he let his gaze dip a fraction, absorbing the shape of her lips, their fullness, their gloss.

'Bo?'

He snapped back to attention, wondering if living the life of a recluse was such a good idea if he started noticing trivial things like his new illustrator's mouth.

He didn't have time for dating; women were a distraction he could do without. His work was all important, finishing this next book on time vital.

'Yeah?'

'I'd kill for a coffee,' she said, sending a pointed glance at the espresso machine on the bench top behind him. 'If you don't mind, that is.'

'No problem. How do you like it?'

For one long, loaded moment, their gazes locked, her lips parted a fraction and he could've sworn the air sizzled with static electricity as if they'd just been through a freak storm.

How do you like it?

He hadn't meant it as a come-on, far from it, and he didn't like the way she stared at him with those mischievous blue eyes, as if assessing him while he grabbed two mugs out of the cupboard and all but slammed them on the granite bench top.

'Strong. Hot. Sweet.'

Wishing she'd stop staring at him as if he was the most fascinating creature, making him feel like he'd sprouted ears and fur, he turned his back on her and busied himself with the coffee, hoping this wasn't a mistake.

He had a high work ethic and a low tolerance level for incompetence; though Tahnee came highly recommended, he didn't like the easy familiarity she'd already slipped into around him: her confident smile, her teasing eyes and the unshakeable feeling that somehow she was laughing at him for being a workaholic author who didn't get out much.

'How many sugars?'

'Two, please. No milk.'

He heard a rustling and crackle of paper bags being opened and he hoped she wasn't pulling out any more surprises. He'd had enough in the last few minutes to last him a while.

Moira had been the perfect co-worker: quiet, dependable and a total non-distraction with her light brown hair, plain features and navy business suits. He'd never had the impulse to study Moira's mouth. No way.

He'd been one hundred per cent focused on work around Moira and they'd been a cohesive team. With Tahnee, he had an awful suspicion that associating teamwork with the gorgeous blonde might lead him to ponder other creative directions altogether, directions he hadn't headed down in a long while, directions that had nothing to do with words or pictures or kids' stories.

'Can I tempt you?'

Bo almost jumped out of his skin as she sneaked up behind him and offered an open paper bag filled with plump croissants, the mouth-watering buttery aroma combining with the fresh, floral scent he'd inhaled earlier as she'd walked into the room.

'Thanks,' he muttered, taking a croissant and turning back to pour the coffee.

This was insane, stupid and counter-productive.

He needed Tahnee Lewis to finish his book; he didn't need her distracting him with an amused expression that appeared permanently etched across her face.

Sighing in resignation, he turned back to find her staring at him with a smug smile as if she knew exactly how annoyed he was and was enjoying every minute.

The woman was a nuisance.

The woman was a curse.

The woman had to save his butt, so, for now, she'd stay.

* * *

Tahnee sipped at her coffee and tried not to stare at her new boss.

Tried and failed.

Little wonder Bo Bradford didn't have a bio and pic on his website. The number of hits he'd get would send the 'net into meltdown.

She watched him fuss around the kitchen, looking for a plate to dump the croissants on—Nina's favourite almond croissants, which she'd thrown into Tahnee's car when she was leaving. She hadn't felt like eating on the drive down.

Lucky for her, considering Bo looked like he could do with a bit of sweetening up. He might look like the hottest guy on the eastern seaboard of Australia, but, boy, did he need to lighten up.

'These smell good,' he said, placing the plate between them and sliding into a seat opposite her. 'Michel's? Never heard of it.'

'It's a small bakery in Stockton, where I live.'

Not just where she lived, her home. She belonged in Stockton; she liked the comfort of knowing everyone in town, she liked the cosy atmosphere and it made her feel secure, a feeling she'd do anything to preserve.

'It won't be a problem, you staying here for a few weeks?'

She bit back a smile. What Mr Nosy was really asking was if she had anyone to miss her in Stockton, namely a significant other.

Well, her boss was entitled to know stuff like that, she supposed, but with her appreciation for a fine-looking guy, she almost wished there was more to it than a professional interest.

Yeah, right, like she needed her grumpy boss to be interested in a fling, while trialling her for the most important job of her career.

'No problem at all. I have an overprotective best friend who quizzed me at length about staying here, a sister who is overseas for a few months and another living in Singapore, but apart from that I'm footloose and fancy-free.'

Tahnee mentally clapped a hand over her mouth.

Why did she say that? Guys who looked like him would probably take it as a come-on. She needed to smarten up her act or she'd be out on her butt along with her sketchbook and charcoals.

He stared at her over the rim of his coffee mug, his steady, green gaze unwavering. 'Good. We don't have time for distractions. I need to get my current book done ASAP.'

'Tight deadline?'

His eyes froze, a peculiar greeny-blue hue, the exact colour of an icy glacier she'd seen on an Alaskan documentary once.

'Exactly,' he said, his flat tone matching his frigid eyes. 'If you've finished your coffee, I'll show you the flat.'

O-kay. Was it something she'd said?

Boy, the guy was prickly. Extremely sexy, but definitely prickly and she hated having to tread on eggshells. She'd never been that type of person, preferring blunt honesty to games, which probably explained why she was eternally single and couldn't hold on to a guy beyond a few dates.

Sad, considering she wouldn't mind the whole hubby, two-point-five kids and a white-picket-fence dream one day. After all, how much more secure could she get than when surrounded by a family she had created?

Finishing her coffee in three quick gulps, she stood up and headed for the sink to rinse her mug. 'I'm ready.'

Anything to diffuse the weird tension that had enveloped them; the atmosphere seemed taut enough since she'd arrived, and when she'd asked him about his book he'd gone cold on her. Just what she needed, a temperamental artist with power over her future.

Turning around, she caught him staring at her butt before he quickly raised his gaze to eye level and she smothered a giggle.

The guy blew hotter and colder than a spring day. First he froze her out; now he looked decidedly flustered in a very uncold way. Cute, considering he had everything she valued in a guy: great pecs and flat abs hugged by a grey T-shirt, lean legs moulded by faded denim, just over six foot, amazing eyes, short back and sides, facial features arranged just right.

Okay, so she was trying to play down the high cheekbones, straight nose, clean jaw and overall symmetry of his face, but hey, she needed to concentrate on work, not her boss's model potential.

'Come on, let's go. I haven't got all day.'

This time, Tahnee couldn't stifle her smile at his barked order and, as she followed him, letting him carry her bags for being such a grump, she did a bit of butt-checking of her own, not surprised it matched the perfection of the rest of him.

Hmm…maybe finding inspiration for her work over the next fortnight wouldn't be so difficult after all.

CHAPTER TWO

Wally stared at his new friend Kaz the Kangaroo. She wasn't like anyone he'd met before. She had a big smile and a great tail! But he wasn't sure if she'd be any good at helping him dig yet. All she seemed to do was talk—a lot—and he wanted to work.
Bo Bradford's blog, Monday.

'Wow, great place.'

Bo dumped Tahnee's bags inside the door and looked up, glad something was going right.

If she liked the flat, maybe she'd stay there for the duration of her time here and he could drop her in a draft of his work first thing every morning and leave her to it.

No distractions.

The key to his success.

'I can't wait to see where you work,' she said, spinning around from the floor-to-ceiling window overlooking the pool and Sydney Harbour beyond. 'Bet it's some room to keep you inspired.'

So much for keeping her out of his work place and not being distracted.

'I like it. Would you like a tour now?'

'Sure.'

She grinned like an excited kid and he wondered if she was this exuberant all the time. She seemed genuinely glad to be here, her buoyant personality grating on him already.

He preferred solitude and valued peace and quiet while he worked. Moira had known that and had fitted in perfectly while he had a nasty feeling the effervescent woman practically bouncing around like Kaz the Kangaroo, his latest creation, would drive him up the wall within the first hour.

Her light touch on his arm startled him. 'Look, this is probably none of my business, but you don't seem too happy to have me here. If you've changed your mind, maybe we can work something out? Perhaps we can work by correspondence—you email me your work and I'll fax the sketches back, something like that?'

He glanced down at her hand, the short fingernails devoid of polish, the bump on her third finger where she obviously rested her pencils. It was the hand of an artist, a creator, someone who would understand him, someone he could work with if he let go of the bad mood that had gripped him since she'd stepped through the back door.

He hadn't been a people person for a while now, and having someone as bright and bubbly as Tahnee show up had him bristling more than he'd anticipated.

He forced a smile, hoping to reassure her.

'I want you here. I need to get a feel for your work first hand and emailing won't cut it for now. I guess losing Moira has thrown me and I'm still trying to get my head around finding a replacement.'

Her answering smile, bright, dazzling and genuine, sent remorse through him; he needed to lighten up.

'Moira was brilliant. I loved how she gave Wally those cute expressions.' She paused, nibbling on her bottom lip. 'I just hope I can fill her shoes.'

'You don't need to fill anyone's shoes. I've seen your work. It speaks for itself, which is why you're here. Now, ready for that tour?'

'Sure,' she said, though Bo glimpsed the uncertainty in her eyes, the slight droop of her mouth.

Tahnee Lewis wasn't as confident as she liked to portray.

Good. That made two of them.

Tahnee felt like Prue the Platypus, one of Bo's creations who entered a different world when she jumped into the creek and swam underwater.

Yeah, she felt exactly like that—amazed, wide-eyed, thrilled—as she followed Bo through his harbour-side mansion, trying not to ogle the beautiful furniture, the wide windows with stunning views and, most of all, the guy showing her around.

This had to be an alternate reality.

Too good to be true.

'This place is amazing,' she said, gaping at an exquisite Pro Hart painting, which brightened up a creamy wall with its vibrant slashes of colour. 'I'm not surprised you get so creative living here.'

'I like it.'

His simple response spoke volumes, considering it was the first time he'd injected any warmth into his voice since she'd arrived.

'How long have you lived here?'

'Five years.'

Okay, he wasn't so big on the sharing personal info thing. No drama. She didn't need to know everything about the guy to work with him, though it would sure help to establish some kind of rapport. She'd keep trying. He had to crack eventually.

'You bought this place before you made it big?'

He'd first hit the bestseller lists four years ago, which meant he'd had a serious advance or ten before that. Or rich rellies.

He stopped suddenly and she pulled up in record time before she slammed into his back—though copping a feel to see if those muscles felt as good as they looked beneath the cotton mightn't be so bad.

'Are you always this nosy?'

'Are you always this defensive?'

He'd turned to face her, his body mere centimetres from hers, bringing new meaning to the phrase 'up close and personal.' She could feel heat radiating off him, drawing her towards him like a magnet, teasing her to close the short gap between them and—

'Want to see my office?'

'Is that the same as seeing your etchings?'

For a split second, she thought she'd gone too far as he stared at her in what could only be termed as shock considering his dilated pupils. Either that, or he was seriously turned on and she doubted that—she would've picked up on it—because, apart from staring at her butt earlier, he acted like she was an unwelcome guest rather than someone he wanted to ravish.

Just as she was about to do some serious back-pedalling—or groveling, depending on how tired he'd grown of her already—he laughed, a low, husky chuckle that rippled over her like a summer's breeze.

'You're nothing like I expected,' he said, a rueful smile transforming his face from good-looking to drop-dead gorgeous in the speed of light.

'Same here.'

And that was an understatement. She'd expected some bearded hermit, maybe sporting the odd fang or two, who howled at the moon and transformed, a bit of a freak who needed privacy to hide his many secrets. Instead, Bo was six-foot-plus of gorgeous male. And then some!

Apart from illustrating children's books, she loved to sketch beautiful things, and right now her fingers fairly itched to pick up a charcoal and transfer Bo onto paper.

His smile faded and he ran a hand over his face, while she hoped he wouldn't put his grumpy mask back in place.

'Look, I'm not a people person. Guess I've been holed up here too long. Sorry if I came on a bit strong before.'

She shrugged, wondering if the surly Bo hadn't been safer than this relaxed, semi-amused Bo.

'Don't worry about it. I'm a country girl at heart and I call it how it is. My friend Nina thinks I'm too blunt, but hey, no point beating around the bush, right?'

'Right.'

His smile was back and it illuminated his face, took five years off it and had her grinning like an idiot right back at him.

Like the loaded moment back in the kitchen when they'd both stared at each other without saying a word, he stared at her now, his eyes studying her, the expression in their green depths unreadable.

'And here we have Wally's digs.'

He broke the spell by throwing open a door on his right and she gasped, enchanted by the room he'd had the audacity to call an office.

'Oh, my,' she said, stepping into a high-ceilinged room as big as her entire flat back home, soaking up the late morning sun that filtered through expansive windows, admiring yet another stunning view of the harbour and the bridge.

She turned a slow three-sixty degrees, eager to explore every book that lined three walls of floor-to-ceiling shelves, impressed by the many book covers framed on the walls. Rich wood combined with bright rugs, light combined with fresh sea air drifting in an open window, and right in the middle of all this splendour stood the guy who'd brought her here, looking more at home here than he had in the rest of the house.

'If I had a place like this to work in, I'd never want to leave,' she said, walking over to his desk near a window, smiling when she saw little figurines of his animal characters sitting atop his hard drive.

'I spend most of my time here.'

He joined her at the desk, radiating a potent mix of heat and pheromones, the kind that called to her like nothing had before.

She really needed to get a date while she was here. Maybe she'd call up the last guy she'd had dinner with in Sydney a while back. Pity she couldn't remember his name.

'I assume you know who these little fellas are?'

She picked up Wally, the fictional rotund wombat who'd launched his kiddie-writer career.

'I do, but why don't you go ahead and introduce me anyway?'

'You're holding my favourite little guy in the entire world. Then this here is Prue the Platypus and Kevin the Koala.'

She laughed as he picked up the cute figurines no bigger than his thumb and danced them across the desk towards her, complete with formal little bows. 'The prickly dude is Eddy?'

'Eddy the Echidna at your service.'

Eddy joined the rest of his mates on the edge of the desk and she picked him up, bringing his snout in close contact with Prue's till the two were smooching.

'Hey! There's none of that stuff in my books.'

'Too bad,' she said, replacing Prue and Eddy in their rightful spots, but with backs to each other as if in a huff. 'Now see what you've done? They've had a lovers' tiff.'

He raised an eyebrow. 'Maybe you should be writing the stories? Seems like you've got one hell of an imagination.'

She blushed at the speculative gleam in his eyes. If he only knew exactly how vivid her imagination was. Right now it had the two of them doing what Prue and Eddy had been doing a second ago, but without stopping.

If she ever had the pleasure of locking lips with sexy Bo, she wouldn't stop at kissing. Not that she was a floozie or anything, but the few times she'd had sex in her life had been lacklustre and boring to say the least.

Where were the screaming orgasms the books promised? Where were the sparks? The erogenous zones? The endless foreplay?

In her dreams, that's where.

Little wonder she stuck to meaty mysteries these days. She left the romance stuff to people who believed in magic, people like Nina, who'd been buying contemporary romances by the truckload since she was a teen.

No, romance wasn't for her. Heck, she'd settle for a feel-good fling right about now, considering what was on offer.

Get real! The guy's your boss and moody to boot. The last thing you need is to bump bits with him. And by the funny way he's staring at you, he's not likely to offer you anything other than your marching orders.

'Having a good imagination helps with creativity,' she said, perching on the side of the desk. 'You'd know all about that.'

His green-eyed stare glowed emerald for a moment

and she blinked, wondering if she'd imagined the speculation there, knowing it wouldn't be the first time she'd imagined a guy's interest and had been let down when she'd had a reality check.

'Sure do. Speaking of which, I hope you can kick-start your imagination a.s.a.p.'

'Uh-huh.'

'I've invented two new characters and they need to slot into this current book. Deadline's in two weeks. Think you can manage it?'

'Easy,' she said, knowing it would be anything but working around a guy as pleasing to the eye as him. 'How do you like to work?'

In a perfect world, his answer would involve the two of them laying by the pool, sipping margaritas while brainstorming, or, better yet, sprawled in the huge king-size bed she'd glimpsed as he'd hurried her past the part of the tour involving his bedroom.

'How about I give you a scene-by-scene layout and you go from there?'

'Great. I'm used to working like that.'

'And for the new characters, I'll add a few more annotations to give you an idea of what I want.'

'No probs.'

Though there was one. How was she meant to concentrate if they worked in the same room?

It hadn't been a problem in the past. She'd always worked from home, enjoying the freedom of being her own boss, the freedom to work in her PJs if she wanted. Somehow, she had a feeling that wouldn't go down too well around here. Not with Bo wavering between grumpy and slightly less than grumpy.

'You can work in here if you like.'

'You sure I won't get in your way? I can work anywhere.'

'Here is fine,' he said, sounding less than enthused about the idea. 'That way, we can get a feel for how each other works, iron out any kinks in the early stages before they become a problem.'

'Okay. When do we start?'

He glanced at his watch, an expensive silver designer number that probably cost more than her rent for a year.

'How about after lunch?'

'Sounds good.'

She waited, unsure whether he expected her to join him or whether he'd relegated her to stay-out-of-the-way status again.

'You're welcome to join me.'

By his flat monotone, she'd be as welcome as a snake at a picnic.

'Thanks, but I'll get settled in and grab something later. Meet you back here at one?'

He nodded and turned back to his desk, effectively dismissing her.

Tahnee shook her head and headed for the flat.

Maybe working with the sexy author wouldn't be a problem after all. If she concentrated on his moody side, the side that wavered back and forth at whim, focusing on work instead of his great bod and handsome face would be a cinch.

CHAPTER THREE

Wally scratched his belly, sat back and watched Kaz flick her long tail from side to side. He reckoned she was doing it on purpose, just to distract him. It was working. With an annoyed growl, he turned away and starting digging harder, his claws making little headway in the dirt.
Bo Bradford's blog, Monday evening.

'MEET MY latest buddies. Kaz the Kangaroo and Kenny the Kookaburra.'

Bo opened the top drawer of his desk and pulled out the cutest imitation kangaroo and kookaburra Tahnee had ever seen.

'They're adorable!'

'They will be if you draw them right,' he said, plonking them into her outstretched hands. 'Kaz is Wally's new mate, his best friend, and I have a feeling Wally's developing a little crush on her. Kenny is the joker of the pack. He eggs everyone on and spends all day laughing at them.'

'I love it,' she said, wondering how such a serious guy could have such a vivid imagination—and wondering if it extended to other facets of his life.

'The kids are going to love it.'

'That's what counts.'

He handed her several cardboard pieces where he'd pasted bits of paper.

'Here are the first three scenes I need illustrated. In the first one, I need Wally to look wary as he meets Kaz while she's sassy and over-confident. In the second, Kaz is showing off and Wally's doing his best to look bored while Kenny laughs his head off. In the third, Wally's sneaking bashful peeks at Kaz, who loves the attention. Is that enough info?'

'You'll see soon enough,' she said, taking the layouts and heading to the huge royal-blue suede couch in the corner, her fingers itching to get started.

'There's a smaller desk over there if you need it. Moira used to work there.'

It figured.

She glanced at the neat-as-a-pin, generic grey desk with its PC, in-tray and standard office chair, and plopped onto the comfy couch.

'I'll be fine over here. I prefer to be comfortable when I work.'

'Suit yourself.'

He shrugged and turned away, but not before she'd seen the bemused look on his face.

So she confused him? What was new?

She confused most guys she came into contact with.

They didn't get her 'honesty is best' policy, especially when applied to their inadequacies. Life was too short to waste mucking about when she hoped to find the right guy eventually.

Not that she was holding her breath.

Tahnee pushed back into the cushions, sighing with pleasure as they moulded around her. Now this was a couch she could work on. Her own at home held similar welcoming properties: supportive yet comfortable, firm yet squishy, just right.

'Are you okay?'

She looked up to find Bo staring at her with more of that confusion she'd come to expect.

'Fine, just getting comfortable.'

'Right,' he said, the corners of his mouth twitching as he ducked behind his computer screen.

'You wouldn't understand,' she muttered, casting surreptitious glances at his state-of-the-art desk with its sleek lines, huge glass top, neat trays and built-in pen holder. His straight-backed ergonomic chair finished the ensemble.

She couldn't work like that, all neat and uptight. In the later stages, when she had to present the final product to the publisher, sure—but now, in the early free-for-all ideas stage? Uh-uh.

Setting Kaz and Kenny on the seat next to her, she rummaged in her bag for sketchpad and charcoals. She'd brought half her work things with her much to Nina's disgust. Her friend had insisted she take more changes of wardrobe, but she'd rather have a larger choice of charcoals than shoes.

Besides, as she'd hoped, Bo didn't look the dress-up-and-entertain type. A guy who kept to himself, valued his privacy enough to keep his pic off his website and practically snapped at her rather than holding a civilised conversation probably didn't throw huge parties, so the several pairs of jeans she'd packed would do just fine.

'Why don't you have a bio on your website?'

She'd wanted to know and now seemed as good a time as any to ask, considering the thought had popped into her head.

'Not relevant to the type of books I sell. Kids don't want to know about me, they want to know when the next instalment of Wally and co. is coming out.'

He didn't raise his head from behind the screen and she hated that. Doris, her foster mum, had taught her to always look someone in the eye, especially when they were talking to you.

Well, if Mr Personality didn't have any manners, she'd just prod him till he reacted.

'But isn't your website a major promotional tool? Wouldn't other professionals in the industry want to know about the man behind the phenomenon?'

'I let my work do the talking.'

Another brush-off. Time to get tough.

'Do you wear a disguise to book signings, too? You know, to let your work do the talking.'

That grabbed his attention as he poked his head around the screen, exasperation warring with annoyance if his frown and thinned lips were any indication.

'I go dressed as Wally. Now, can I get back to work?'

'You're kidding, right?'

Either the guy had a serious personality disorder, which prevented him from letting the world see him for who he was, or he was hiding something. She'd bet a year's worth of almond croissants it was the latter.

'I value my privacy and the kids don't care. End of story.'

'That's what you think,' she said as he ducked behind the screen again, muttering something she couldn't hear.

'You're serious, aren't you?'

'Uh-huh,' he said, the brittle edge to his voice signalling he was fast running out of patience.

Well, too bad.

She liked knowing who she worked with. It gave her a better feel for the characters and ultimately produced a better end result.

'You're not a criminal on the run?'

'No.'

'Are you agoraphobic?'

'No.'

At least he was responding, even if he wouldn't look at her. She took it as a sign of encouragement.

'I know. You've got a bunny boiler after you.'

At last, some attention as his head snapped up from behind the screen. 'A what?'

'The type of woman who becomes obsessed with the guy she fancies. You know, like in that movie where the scorned mistress goes into the guy's home and puts his kids' rabbit on the stove and—'

'I get the picture.' He held up both hands as if trying

to ward her off. Like that was going to work. 'Don't you ever shut up?'

'Only when I get the truth,' she said, twirling a charcoal nub between thumb and forefinger like a baton leader. 'If we're going to work together, I need to know what makes Bo Bradford tick. I need to know what inspires you, what gives you the creative edge over the competition—basically, who you are. That way, I can get a real feel for your work and produce the kind of pictures you want.'

'That's a crock.'

He stood up, folded his arms in classic defensive posture and glared at her. 'Moira worked with me for years and didn't pry half as much as you.'

'Moira, Moira, Moira.' She put on her best little girl's voice, though she stopped short of poking her tongue out at him. 'In case you haven't noticed, I'm not Moira. And by the look of that prim and proper desk, I'll never be anything like Moira, so get over it. I'm here to work with the best and that's what I intend to produce for you, too. If you work with me, as in two people giving and taking. Think you can do that?'

His eyes narrowed to green slits, shooting enough fiery daggers to scorch her to cinders on the spot.

'You do realise I can fire you right now?'

A tide of panic washed over her, but she ignored it. She had a feeling bossy Bo was all bark and no bite.

'I don't think you'd want to do that, what with your deadline in two weeks and these new characters to incorporate and my outstanding reputation and—'

'Just get on with it.'

He sat down and hid behind his screen again, but not before she'd seen the worried look flash across his handsome face.

For a guy who faced deadlines all the time, he was acting mighty strange about this one, almost as if it were life and death. Another Bo Bradford mystery to solve…goody!

With an extra-loud exasperated sigh—to tell Bo he might have won the battle but the war was only just beginning—she tucked her feet under her, rested her sketchbook on her lap and studied Kenny's pointy beak.

Bo had secrets—plenty of them, by the looks of things—and if there was one thing she liked more than illustrating, it was solving mysteries. Unfortunately for him, she was darn good at it, too.

So let him give her the brush-off, let him go all recalcitrant on her.

She'd find out what was biting his butt eventually.

It took a superhuman effort for Bo to concentrate on the screen and fill it with words. Whether those words actually made sense or not was another matter but right now it took all his willpower to write and not cross his office to throttle Tahnee.

He knew she'd be trouble the first second he laid eyes on her, but he had had no idea how much.

She was inquisitive, pushy, brash and way too confident for her own good. And she had an annoying habit of nibbling her bottom lip while she concentrated that drove him to distraction.

'How's it coming along?'

He frowned and stood up, needing to stretch, needing to do something other than snap at her for distracting him with her inane chatter for the umpteenth time in the last hour.

'Okay. I've managed four pages'—of crap. 'How about you? Can I take a look?'

'Sure.'

She stretched, linking her hands and reaching overhead, pulling her T-shirt tight over her breasts and exposing a band of flat, tanned midriff. Great. She was disruptive enough without him noticing her impressive physical attributes.

'Here, come and have a look.'

She picked up several bits of paper and patted the seat next to her and he had no option but to sit, when the last thing he needed in his current aggravated state was to waste more time checking up on her when he'd rather be working.

'Well?'

He riffled through the pictures, admiration mingling with relief.

She was good. Very good. Better than Moira and that was saying something, considering Moira had worked with the best in England before spending the last four years with him.

'Aren't you going to say something? I'm having a minor conniption over here.'

He looked up at her, surprised to see genuine concern. 'You might not be anything like Moira, but you're sure sounding like her. Conniption is definitely a Moira word.'

She waved her hand in his face as if trying to erase his words.

'Never mind all that. Tell me what you think about the pictures.'

He reached out to reassure her without thinking, laying a hand on her arm, the kind of impersonal yet reassuring touch he'd give to anybody. But Tahnee wasn't anybody. She was a vibrant, stunning young woman and she had him more bothered than he'd been in years.

He dropped his hand quickly. 'They're great. I'm very impressed.'

'Really?'

The hope he glimpsed in her eyes had him feeling like an ogre. Perhaps he had been a bit tough on her earlier? After all, she had a point about the whole 'getting to know each other to work better' thing.

'Really. Now, how about dinner? I'm cooking.'

It wasn't a big deal. He cooked for himself every night.

'But it's still early…' She trailed off, glancing out the window at the growing dusk and looking back at him in surprise. 'We must've been at it for a while.'

'Four hours, give or take an hour.'

'Wow.'

She flipped her sketchbook shut and slid the charcoal into a box, a strange expression flitting across her face.

'Is something wrong?'

She shook her head. 'I guess I thought it would take me a while to get comfortable here. You know, get into the swing of things. I'm pretty quick when I get into the zone back home, but I never expected it to happen so quickly here.'

He knew exactly what she meant and for a brief second it felt good to be on the same wavelength as somebody. Working with Moira had been somewhat different: she'd taken his scenes, turned her back on him for the day and barely spoken, often sliding the completed work into his in-tray the next morning if she had taken it home.

Tahnee was on a similar plane. She might talk more, but she understood the thrill of losing yourself in your work, when time became irrelevant and hours passed in mere minutes. He loved being in the zone and it looked like he'd met his match.

Figuratively speaking, of course.

'I'm glad you're comfortable here,' he said, handing back her sketches. 'And I'm even gladder you can produce that quality of work so quickly. You're very talented.'

'That's what they all say.'

She sent him a coy glance from beneath her lashes, smiling broadly when he shuffled like a rabbit ready to bolt.

'Let me guess. Moira didn't flirt with you, either.'

'Hell, no!'

The thought of forty-five-year-old Moira, with her short, mousy bob, wire-rimmed specs, navy business suits and no-nonsense shoes, flirting with him seemed as incongruous as him heading back to the world of finance to earn a bob.

Not a chance.

Tahnee laughed and stood in one fluid movement, her lithe body showing little sign of cramp from being in one position for so long.

'Well, if I get out of hand, you know what you have to do.'

'What's that?'

'Spank me.'

While he struggled with deciphering whether she was kidding or not, she sashayed out the door, leaving him torn between wanting to sack her on the spot or holing up in his room till she left him in peace at the end of the fortnight.

'This fettuccine carbonara is sensational,' Tahnee said, twirling a long length of pasta around her fork and mopping up the thick, creamy sauce with it. 'Where did you learn to cook like this?'

Bo raised his wineglass and for a second she thought he wouldn't answer. Darn the man and his secrets.

'I spent six months in Italy years ago. I got hooked then.'

'That must've been exciting,' she said, forking pasta into her mouth and sighing in contentment.

She loved food and, courtesy of a fast metabolism and her height, could indulge her passion on a regular basis. However, her culinary masterpieces consisted of roast lamb and veggies followed by a fresh fruit Pavlova. Not exactly world-class cuisine.

'Yeah, it was. My brother and I toured the whole

country.' He came to an abrupt halt as if he'd said too much.

She was getting tired of the big secrecy thing real quick. The only way to get him to talk was to push.

'You have a brother?'

She laid down her fork and reached for a chunk of panne cotta bread to mop up the little sauce remaining in her bowl, trying to keep her question casual when, in fact, she was dying to get an insight into this enigmatic guy.

'Yeah.'

'And?'

Gee, would this guy ever give her more than the barest of polite answers? She'd known he was a recluse but, boy, could he use with a year's worth of social-etiquette classes.

He sipped at his shiraz, staring into the wine before he finally laid down his glass.

'We're not that close.'

'Bad case of sibling rivalry, huh?'

'Nothing that interesting. We're just different people now.'

'You must've been close at one point to travel to Italy together?'

He glowered at her, his green eyes flinty.

'Don't you ever get tired of prying into other people's business?'

'No,' she said, flashing him a broad smile while wondering how far she could push him.

This was interesting stuff. Much better than eating in silence with the occasional polite 'pass the Parmesan, please' or 'more garlic bread?' thrown in.

With an exasperated sigh, he leaned back in his chair and folded his arms.

'We used to work together in our dad's financial company, one of the largest in Australia. Brennan and I were pretty good buddies, but we don't dig the same things any more. He's into making money at any cost and living the high life, I've finally followed my dream and done the creative thing. He's Dad's golden boy, and I'm fine with that, though we just don't see eye to eye any more. My dad respects my need for solitude, but Brennan doesn't get it. He can't understand why I like to be holed up here writing rather than out drinking and partying.'

Wow. She stared at Bo in surprise, more because he'd spoken more than two words to her than the information he'd imparted.

'You were in finance before you were published? That's a big career change.'

For the first time since she'd arrived, he smiled, a fully fledged grin that set her pulse thundering in response. The guy was seriously gorgeous when he wasn't being the silent tyrant boss or hiding behind his grumpy mask.

'Yeah, a huge change. I can actually use my brain for manipulating animal figures rather than tossing around financial figures. It's great.'

Encouraged by his smile—and the fact that he seemed to have stopped biting her head off for asking so many probing questions—she said, 'So what prompted you to make the change?'

'Kay.'

His smile faded somewhat and he took a sip of wine.

For some strange reason, hearing him say a woman's name woke a little green-eyed monster she never knew existed. To make matters worse, the annoying monster clawed out, sending a sharp stab of jealousy through her.

Dousing the monster with a good dumping of common sense, she said, 'Kay?'

'Ex-girlfriend. We met through work, hung out a lot, thought hooking up would be a good move, but we were too different. She pointed out that I was more wrapped up in the jottings I made in a notebook I carried around with me than in her, and she was right. There were no hard feelings. In fact, I was relieved when she dumped me to take off with our managing director, even grateful when I realised she'd given me a long-overdue wake-up call. I took those jottings, drafted my first book, got an agent and the rest…well, you probably know the rest, a snoop like you.'

His words didn't bear any malice and she grinned at him, the green-eyed monster picking up some pom-poms and doing a happy dance. The woman sounded like a mercenary cow, and from where Tahnee sat—opposite an intelligent, creative, gorgeous guy—it was her loss.

'More wine?'

'No, thanks.'

Her head already had a fuzzy tinge and, combined with her feeling sorry for her jilted boss, the cosy ambience of the kitchen and the slight crush she'd developed on Bo in less than twenty-four hours, the last thing she needed was more alcohol. 'Though can I ask a question?'

'Haven't you asked enough?' He spoke without rancour, his eyes defrosting to a warmer green.

'You said your family's finance company is large? I've never heard of the Bradfords.'

Okay, so she was sneaky, but he'd opened up to her more than she'd expected over the last few minutes—why stop when he was on a roll?

'Bradford is a pseudonym.'

'Oh.'

Obvious, considering his obsession over privacy.

'Then I guess it's no use me asking what your real name is?'

He topped up his wineglass, a small smile playing around his mouth as he ignored her.

'Come on, Bo, you know I'm naturally curious.'

She put on her best wheedling voice and his smile turned to outright laughter.

'You're naturally *nosy* and you said one question.'

'That hardly counted as a question. Give me your real name and I promise I'll stop.'

She held up two fingers to her forehead in a Scout's salute. At least, that's what she hoped it looked like. Otherwise, he might take it as a very rude sign.

'Bogart.'

She leaned forward, not sure if she'd heard correctly. 'Pardon?'

'My real name is Bogart.'

Hmm...she wasn't surprised he used the diminutive Bo. Much sexier, though she guessed Humphrey did it for the older generation.

'Your first name, you mean?'

He nodded. 'Mum had a thing for *Casablanca*.'

'No kidding.' She fiddled with the stem of her empty wineglass, wondering if she could push him just a tad further. 'So it's Bogart...?'

'That's your quota of questions for today, Ms Nosy. Now, would you like a coffee?'

He stood and headed for the sink, the conversation closed.

Not that she could blame him. Nina would've had a hissy fit if she'd seen how Tahnee had pushed him tonight. In fact, she'd been pushing him all day and for someone she could've sworn didn't want her here, he'd taken it surprisingly in his stride.

She valued blunt honesty and fostered an intense curiosity for mysteries—that didn't mean everyone else did. Overall, he'd been a good sport and she really needed to give the guy a break.

With that in mind, she stood up, dumped her bowl in the sink and said, 'You wash, I'll dry, okay?'

'Fine.'

Her decision to tone down her personality and be nice didn't last very long as she saw his solemn mask slide back into place. Picking up a dishcloth from the oven handle, she eyed his tempting butt and flicked it with the cloth ever so lightly.

'What the hell?'

He swivelled so fast that water and soap suds flew everywhere and she squealed, swatting away flying bubbles and water droplets, creating a diversion.

He didn't buy it.

'Did you just flick my butt?'

She struggled to keep a straight face, she really did, but fighting losing battles wasn't one of her strong points.

'When I pulled the dishcloth off the rack, it might've skimmed you. Accidentally, of course,' she added, knowing her burgeoning grin wouldn't convince him.

It didn't.

'I guess I should be grateful it wasn't your hands,' he said, a glimmer of a smile working its way through his grim expression.

'Believe me, you'll know if my hands ever find their way there,' she said, turning away with sudden embarrassment and heading for the table, trying to appear busy clearing it.

What had she been thinking?

That's the last time she'd drink around him. No telling what she might do, considering she couldn't get the image of her hands on his butt out of her head now that she'd thought about it.

'Tahnee?'

'Yeah?'

She didn't look up from the table, gathering the salt-and-pepper shakers, the olive oil bottle and the parmesan cheese, rearranging them like a general organising field placements for his troops and wishing the floor would open up and swallow her now.

'You're an inquisitive woman and I bet you know a lot about me, such as the fact I value my privacy and have lived like a recluse for the last five years?'

'Yeah?'

She continued to fiddle with the cutlery, intense embarrassment at what she'd just done seeping through her body till she wanted to bolt from the kitchen, from the house, and never come back.

'I haven't dated much in that time.'

'So?'

She kept her answer non-committal, wishing the sandstone-tiled floor would crack open and swallow her whole.

'Well, you shouldn't push a guy like that.'

'I don't know what came over me,' she said, feeling like the worst kind of fool and hoping this didn't affect her chances of securing long-term work with him.

She sensed him come up behind her a second too late as his hands settled on her waist and turned her around till her startled gaze met his serious one.

'Good. In that case, you'll understand that I don't know what's come over me, either,' he said, a split second before his lips locked on hers.

CHAPTER FOUR

Wally and Kaz finished dinner, then stretched out by the camp-fire. They drank mugs of hot billy tea and told stories. But Wally couldn't concentrate. Kaz kept smiling at him and he didn't like it. It confused him. He went to bed, but when he said goodnight to Kaz, she blew him a kiss. He waddled away, his tummy feeling funny.
Bo Bradford's blog, late Monday night.

TAHNEE had never been kissed like this before.

She'd had the perfunctory goodnight kiss, the sweet-but-no-spark kiss, the pseudo-passionate kiss and the comfortable-as-old-socks kiss.

But never in her twenty-five years had she had this kind of impulsive, opportunistic, toe-curling clash of lips that ignited every latent hormone in her body.

She came alight; there was no other way to describe it as Bo's lips coaxed hers with a steady, sensual assault. He didn't have to do much coaxing as she opened her mouth, wanting him to taste her, to tease her, to kiss her like she'd never been kissed before.

He deepened the kiss, sucking her bottom lip, nibbling it, flickering his tongue along it as her body melted against him in a hot heap of mushy bones and muscles. Every inch of her skin craved his with an intensity that left her breathless as she slid her hands under the bottom edge of his T-shirt and encountered firm, warm skin covering hard muscle.

A low groan started in the back of his throat, a sexy sound that prompted her to slide her hands ever so slowly downwards, toying with the waistband of his jeans.

'Hell.'

He broke the kiss, staring at her like she'd lost her mind. Not fair, considering he'd been the one to start it.

But she had been the one with the roving hands.

Yeah, well, she couldn't help it if she was a tactile person. It came with the creativity gene.

He's creative, too.

Which had her fingers itching to explore him all over again.

'That's some goodnight kiss,' she said, slipping out of his embrace and thrusting her hands in her jean pockets as if sharing sizzling kisses with her boss was par for the course.

'That should never have happened,' he snapped, running a hand through his hair; she noticed that it shook.

Good, so she wasn't the only one rattled.

Pasting a fake smile in place, she said, 'Hey, don't

beat yourself up over it. Us creative types have a lot of crazy impulses. It's no big deal.'

Tell that to her heart, which had kick-started the minute his mouth locked on hers and hadn't slowed down since.

'I don't do impulsive. And I sure as hell don't go around kissing women I barely know.'

His lips compressed in a thin, hard line and she wondered how he could stand there and act so darn self-righteous when all she wanted to do was jump him and pick up where they'd left off.

She shrugged, eyeing the doorway. Time to make a hasty exit while she still had some dignity left. Glossing over the kiss was one thing, experiencing action replay—with her kissing him this time—another.

'Like I said, it's no biggie. I'm pretty cute, you couldn't help yourself. These things happen.'

'No, they don't. Not to me. I'm sorry.'

He glared at her as if this was all her fault, which technically it was, considering she'd flicked him first.

But hey, she'd only wanted to get him to loosen up a bit, to lose the uptight attitude and the grim face, not kiss her silly.

Maybe it was the wine, maybe a tummy full of pasta or maybe it was the kiss to end all kisses, but she could've hung around the kitchen all night staring down the angry guy who looked like he wanted to strangle her rather than kiss her ever again.

'We need to call it a night,' he said, bracing his arms against the bench top and leaning backwards, highlighting a great set of biceps and a chest she'd almost had the pleasure of exploring in greater detail.

'I guess we should.'

She didn't move.

Her mind transmitted the message to her legs, but it somehow got lost in the translation, considering it had to bypass her lower regions, which were throbbing with want.

Seconds passed, maybe minutes—she had no idea as they stood there, gazes locked, fury and fire in his, challenge and uncertainty in hers.

She'd never been kissed like that before, and by her boss, no less.

Her boss.

And just like that, the message finally transmitted to her legs and she took a step back.

'See you in the morning. What time do you want to start?'

'I'm an early riser. How does nine suit you?'

'Fine, but that's not early.'

'I will have had a swim and put in two hours by then.'

She grimaced. She'd never been a morning person.

'Nine is fine.'

It wasn't the thought of getting up early that was the problem as much as the thought of spending another thirteen days in his company that had her on tenterhooks.

'Good. See you then.'

'Right.'

He hadn't moved, his casual pose showing off the body that had tempted her to lose it a few minutes ago—

long legs, broad shoulders, great arms—and she briefly wondered if he was doing it on purpose. Sort of like showing her what she was missing out on.

Well, too bad. She wasn't the one who'd come to her senses first and ended that kiss.

Though she should have been.

Spinning on her heel, she made it to the door before he spoke.

'That kiss was a big mistake and it will never happen again.'

'Never is a long time,' she said, tossing him a teasing look over her shoulder before walking out the door.

Bo paced his office.

He'd tried booting up his computer and working: nothing.

He'd tried reading the latest sci-fi release from his favourite author: he'd read the same paragraph six times.

He'd even tried rolling the weird metal stress balls Moira had given him as a going-away present in the palm of his hand: he'd almost ended up flinging them against the wall.

Nothing alleviated his frustration or his anger.

He'd kissed Tahnee.

A stupid, spur-of-the-moment impulse that, even now, he couldn't quite believe he'd given into. He prided himself on being in control and his ability to focus on the task at hand, which right now was finishing the book that would catapult his career into the stratosphere.

It had to be the close proximity.

He'd been holed up in here for the last few months, working fourteen-hour days, trying to fulfil his latest contract: the book that would launch him in the competitive overseas market. Though, in reality, he'd locked himself away for the last five years and focused on swapping one life for another. While his work might be blossoming, the seclusion had addled his brain, resulting in him jumping the first attractive woman to come near him in years.

Damn it, he was lucky she was so understanding. Then again, he probably wouldn't have kissed her if she hadn't flicked him with the dishcloth. A bold move, a sassy move, the kind of unpredictability he found somehow appealing, possibly because she was the complete antithesis of him, a boring stiff who buried himself in work.

He stopped short and sank onto the couch, picking up the sketches Tahnee had completed that afternoon, flicking through them, not surprised to find himself smiling by the end. She'd captured Kaz perfectly with a cheeky grin and huge, doe-like eyes and long eyelashes, giving the kangaroo an innocent, yet teasing, glint. Poor Wally didn't stand a chance.

Just like him if he didn't get his ass into gear and get this book done without further complications.

For that's all that kiss was in reality, an unwanted complication, a lapse in judgement, a blip on the radar.

Apart from craving complete quiet while he worked, he'd stopped socialising for a reason. Relationships were complicated and distracting and every woman he'd ever been involved with had expected more than he was willing to give. After Kay, he'd tried to keep dating casual, but women didn't do casual very well, they always wanted more. Whereas his characters liked him just the way he was.

A kiss could lead to expectations on Tahnee's part and it annoyed the hell out of him that he'd slipped up like that.

Come tomorrow, he'd be all business again and put his stupid, momentary lapse out of his mind.

For now, he'd update his blog, anything to get his brain concentrating on getting words from his fingertips to the screen and not on the fact that a gorgeous woman lay in bed, probably in something recklessly skimpy, less than twenty metres away.

Jeez.

His fingers clattered on the keyboard, his eyes glued to the screen, but his mind refused to come to the party and he logged off within five minutes, heading to bed in a huff.

An annoyed-as-hell, frustrated huff.

Tahnee sat cross-legged on her bed and picked up her mobile, flipping it over and over. She could ring Nina, but then she'd be likely to blurt out what had happened with Bo in the kitchen earlier tonight and she couldn't comprehend it yet, let alone articulate it.

Maybe she'd send an SMS instead—something along the lines of SOS?

Ever since Karl had bought Nina a new fancy slimline mobile for her birthday, her friend had been texting madly, preferring to SMS rather than chat. However, trying to type a message using the tiny mobile keys to describe her bizarre day would take far too long. Besides, what could she say?

That her boss was a moody, grim-reaper type who looked ready to lop her head off with his scythe for asking too many questions?

That he was an uptight hermit who needed to loosen up a little? Or a lot, as the case may be.

That she'd provoked him into kissing her when she could see it was the last thing he'd wanted to do?

She'd seen it the minute he broke the kiss, anger flaring in his eyes, his lips settling into their residual thin line. She'd been tempted to bait him further, but his grim expression, combined with his frigid apology, had told her she'd pushed him enough for one day. After all, she needed this job more than anything.

So her boss was intriguing, talented, sexy and kissed like a dream. She needed to forget the minor aberration of the kitchen kiss and focus on work, on convincing him he couldn't live without her for his bestselling books.

But, darn it, she couldn't get him out of her head.

She'd taken a long, hot bath in lavender crystals to relax after making it back to the flat—it hadn't worked.

She'd tried reading a few pages of the best mystery novel ever—it hadn't worked.

She'd tried meditating, which she did on the odd occasion to unwind—it hadn't worked.

In fact, the meditation had been her worst effort as every time she tried to visualise a quiet, peaceful spot,

Bo would pop into the picture and she'd remember how he'd tasted—warm and fruity from the wine—and how he'd held her—nice and tight and pressed up against all those yummy muscles—and her relaxation was shot.

The more she tried meditating, the hotter and more worked up she became. She really needed a date soon if she had designs on her dour boss.

Biting her lower lip, she toyed with the keypad, torn between wanting to give Nina a little gossip or a lot. Apart from when it came to Tahnee's love life, her friend didn't possess half the insatiable curiosity she did, always poking her nose into other people's business as Bo had been quick to point out.

She couldn't help it. Maybe it was a genetic thing? She'd never find out now and, for the first time in ages, the hot sting of tears burned her eyes as she wished her mum or Doris were here.

She barely remembered her mum other than the great cuddles she used to give, smelling of toasted cinnamon, but Doris had been good to chat things over with, always ready with a pragmatic word or objective viewpoint.

Boy, could she do with some objectivity now.

She needed someone to tell her, 'Yeah, your boss is attractive, but so what?'

She needed to hear, 'So he kissed you, big deal, move on, get a life.'

Most of all, she needed to hear, 'If you botch up this job, you'll endanger your dream.'

Sighing, she popped the phone in her bedside drawer

and slipped beneath the cotton covers, not ready for Nina's version of the Spanish Inquisition if she texted her.

Not that she'd get much sleep.

She hadn't been this wound up in a long time. The guys she'd dated in the past had been interesting enough, but none had lit her fire like Bo had with that one unexpected kiss. A totally alien concept, considering she preferred to get to know a guy first and the attraction tended to grow from there.

She'd never had an instant wham-bam, in-your-face sexual attraction before and it had her tied up in knots. Usually light-hearted and flirty with guys, she couldn't do that any more with Bo, courtesy of their kiss; he might misconstrue the slightest bit of teasing, and where would they end up then?

In bed, having sensational sex?

Her eyes squeezed shut to block out the image, only to snap open a second later when the erotic pictures filtering across her mind intensified.

She never did this, picturing herself having sex with a guy she'd only just met, not to mention lusting after a work colleague.

It was crazy.

It was dangerous.

Worst of all, it left her with an incredible lust for a guy who should be off-limits.

Work was the answer. If she stayed focused on work and getting the job done right, her irrational instant crush on Bo would fade into the background. They could pretend like the kiss from heaven never happened.

She could do this.

No more dishcloth flicking, no more ogling his butt—or biceps or pecs or abs—keep flirting to a minimum. Concentrate on sketching Wally, Kaz and crew, dazzle Bo with her illustrating skills and keep her mind on the job twenty-four/seven.

Snuggling into bed, she smiled, turned onto her side and let her eyelids flutter shut. Now she had a definite plan of action, she could face whatever bossy Bo had to dish out and more.

Starting first thing in the morning, she'd show him her new ultra-professional side.

She could do it.

Now, if only she could forget the way he kissed…

CHAPTER FIVE

Wally had a lot of work to do. He'd fallen behind thanks to Kaz and her constant chatter. He was grumpier than usual and now he'd been invited to some stupid party down by the water-hole. What was worse, he'd probably have to invite her just to be nice. Why him?
Bo Bradford's blog, Tuesday.

'DAMN IT.'

Tahnee looked up from her sketchpad, where she'd kept her head buried for the last few hours, determinedly not looking Bo's way. Wombat with a sore head wouldn't come close to describing how grumpy he was this morning.

He'd barely spoken to her, banging away at his keyboard like a man possessed and replying to her questions regarding work in short, snapped syllables.

She should be grateful. If this was how he reacted after one kiss, she'd hate to see him if he really lost his head and went wild.

'What's up?'

He ignored her for a moment and she considered Frisbeeing one of her pads at him.

He really was the most rude, gloomy, insufferable man she'd ever met and, for the life of her, she couldn't understand how she could find him remotely attractive.

Though he did have a great body and a sensational smile, on the too-few occasions she'd seen it so far.

Sitting back in his chair, he locked his hands behind his head and sent her an exasperated stare.

'I forgot about this boring publishing awards thing on tonight. My agent just sent me an email and said I have to go.'

'And that's a problem because…?'

Though she already knew the answer to that one. Mr Reclusive took himself way too seriously and if he treated her like a constant interruption he had to endure, she could only imagine what he'd be like socialising at a fancy do.

'I don't have time for it.'

She could've agreed with him and gone back to her drawing, but where was the fun in that?

'Perhaps you should make time. Being an author isn't just about creating, it's about marketing and promotion and putting yourself out there. And I'd hazard a guess that if your agent says it's important, it is.'

His eyes narrowed to green slits, his almost-permanent frown in place. 'Do you bother with all that mundane stuff? "Putting yourself out there"?'

She shook her head, wishing he could go for his

night out now and leave her in peace for the rest of the day. She'd get a heck of a lot more work done without his brooding presence distracting her.

'I'm not an author. No one's interested in schmoozing with the illustrator, they want the person who links the words into magical sentences and makes a bucketload of moola, not some artist who gets a kick out of drawing funky little pictures for kids.'

He didn't respond, staring at her like she'd recited one of his prize-winning books from memory. His intense stare didn't waver and he leaned forward, making her squirm under his scrutiny.

'You're wrong.'

'About what?'

He hit print on his keyboard, crossed to the printer and grabbed a sheet of paper before walking over to the couch and handing her a copy of an email.

'People in the industry are interested in the illustrators. I'm surprised you haven't been to one of these bashes before.'

'Not interested.'

She waved away the email, trying to act like she got invited to posh publishing dos every day when, in fact, she'd only been invited to one before, but had come down with gastro at the last minute and couldn't go. Not that she'd minded terribly. She had a feeling denim wouldn't be entirely suitable anyway.

He sat next to her and all but slapped the email on her sketchpad.

'Neither am I, but if I have to go, you do, too.'

'Oh, no, I don't.'

She didn't glance at the email invitation, preferring to send him the odd dagger or ten with her eyes.

'This is a professional evening. While you're working for me, I expect you to act like a professional and that includes accompanying me to this.'

He jabbed at the email on her pad, the paper making sharp, crinkling noises, the same type of noise it would make when she screwed it up into a ball and lobbed it in his wastepaper basket.

'No.'

Where did he get off telling her to act professional when he was the one who'd kissed her last night?

Okay, so she was trying to forget that incident and concentrate on work and it wouldn't work to her advantage if she flung it in his face now, but, boy, was she tempted.

'You will find all the details here, including the dress code.'

He spoke as if he hadn't heard her response, his gaze flicking over her faded denim hipsters and 'I RULE' pink T-shirt. 'And if you don't have anything suitable to wear, you can have two hours off this afternoon to go shopping.'

'You're mad!'

She jumped up from the couch and stalked to the window, needing to put some distance between them before she did something silly, like shove his invitation up his expensive cashmere cable-knit.

'Not yet, but I will be if you continue to carry on like this.'

His voice had risen and she whirled to face him,

ready to give him a piece of her mind, when he held up his hands as if in surrender.

'Look, I know this evening will be pretty boring but I thought it might be a great opportunity for you to meet some industry heavyweights. Get to know some people. It can only help your career long term, whatever happens at the end of our two weeks' working together. What do you think?'

She thought it sucked. Injecting enthusiasm into her voice, she said, 'Okay, you've convinced me with all your perfectly logical, rational arguments. I'll go. Thanks for asking.'

'No problem.'

He turned away and returned to his desk and she headed back to the couch, picking up the invitation that had slithered to the floor. 'How formal is this cocktail dress code?'

He sat behind his desk, the tiny crease between his brows deepening as he pondered her question.

'The girls don't wear long dresses, just those mid-calf thingies.'

She sent him a rueful grin. 'Thanks for the fashion tip. I'll make sure I grab an appropriate thingy later on this afternoon.'

His mouth twitched and she wished he'd laugh for once, a genuine, roaring outburst or even a more subdued chuckle.

Gee, if he was this sociable tonight, she was in for a real treat. Not.

'We'll leave at eight,' he said, effectively dismissing

her as he returned to clattering on his keyboard—she resisted the urge to send him a salute.

So her boss only saw her as some sort of poor, country nobody who needed an introduction into the big, bad world of publishing?

Well, she'd show him.

An hour or so later, Tahnee was ready to give up. Even chatting for fifteen minutes on the phone to Nina while she shopped hadn't calmed her down and she was ready to find a big, black garbage bag, rip some neck- and armholes and see how Mr Grumpy liked that outfit better than her jeans.

How could finding one dress be this difficult? With a plethora of boutiques to choose from, she'd managed to bypass every single one of them: too pretentious, too expensive, too daggy.

She trudged up the main street of Rose Bay, feet dragging, wishing she had genie powers and could blink the perfect dress into her wardrobe, when she saw it— a poky vintage clothing shop tucked between a vegan café and a day spa.

However, it wasn't the shop that grabbed her attention as much as the dress in the window: a stunning ice-blue Marilyn Monroe-style dress with a halter neck, cinched waist and flaring, pleated skirt.

Suddenly, in that split second, a confirmed jeans girl fell in love…with a dress.

Hurrying into the shop lest the dress vanish like a figment of her imagination, she pounced on the bewildered shop assistant, made frantic hand signals towards the dress and had whipped off her clothes in the dressing room in under a minute.

It probably wouldn't fit.

It would probably make her hips look huge and her tummy bulge.

It was perfect.

As Tahnee stared at herself in the mirror, she couldn't help but grin. She'd never owned anything like it. The dress had to possess magical qualities because no way did she look this good. And the colour…it made her eyes sparkle and her skin glow and made her feel a million dollars.

Oh.

Sighing, she reached for the price tag, aware that vintage shops weren't usually expensive but this was Rose Bay and price went hand in hand with the name.

Squeezing her eyes shut and peeking at the tag through a half-squint, she saw two zeros and her heart sank. No way would she spend hundreds of dollars on a dress she'd probably only wear once. However, as she opened her other eye, her heart danced—there was only a measly little one in front of the zeros.

For a hundred bucks, the dress was a steal and she shimmied out of it, hung it on the peg and pulled her jeans and top back on, feeling almost let down. Denim was where she was at, but apparently satin was in a league of its own.

'I'll take it,' she said, thrusting her money at the young shop assistant who stared at her with fear.

The poor girl probably didn't see too many demented women in hipsters barging into the shop on a mission.

Once the dress had been wrapped in tissue paper and bagged—very upmarket for vintage—Tahnee sent a glorious smile the assistant's way and strutted out of the store, pleased with her purchase and eager for tonight to roll around.

If Bo saw her only as an annoying, nosy, temporary employee he'd engaged, it was time to show him just how engaging she could be.

CHAPTER SIX

Kevin the Koala was throwing a big party down at the water-hole and everyone was invited. Fairy lights hung in the gum trees, lanterns swung from the branches and Prue the Platypus had made fresh lemonade for everyone. There was even music blaring from the lyre-bird big band. Wally was having a great time, then Kaz asked him to dance and the party got even better.
Bo Bradford's blog, Tuesday evening.

TAHNEE caught sight of Bo striding across the foyer and her heart somersaulted. He looked incredible in a white silk shirt highlighting his tan, a black pinstripe suit and an open black bow tie setting off the combination to perfection. However, she'd seen fancy suits before, had dated guys who wore them before, but no guy had ever looked this good, this delicious.

Saliva pooled in her mouth and she quickly swallowed. She'd gone to far too much trouble to drool all over her Marilyn dress now.

Stepping out of the shadows, she fixed a smile on her face, hoping it hid her nerves. She wanted his approval; heck, she craved it with every cell in her moisturised body.

Though her foster parents, Doris and Stan, had done their best to reassure her she belonged, she'd never stopped seeking approval from everyone around her growing up: theirs, the teachers, friends. It was a major part of why she'd stayed in Stockton all these years. Familiarity bred security; for an awkward kid who'd craved it her entire life, it meant everything.

She knew the exact moment Bo spotted her. His feet stopped, his jaw dropped and his eyes rounded into huge, green, bottomless pools.

'Wow,' he breathed, his gaze starting at her silver spangly sandals and working slowly upward, lingering on her waist cinched with a *diamanté* heart and quickly flicking over her breasts. 'You're beautiful.'

You're beautiful.

His words affected her more than she cared to admit. For a girl who'd craved affection her whole life, hating the uncertainty of not knowing her real family, living with the fear of losing her adopted one, she'd never felt beautiful, even though Doris and Stan had done their best to assure her she was.

Funny, cheeky, bold, were all terms she'd been labelled with growing up, but no one had called her beautiful.

Until now.

And though she knew the words probably didn't mean much to him and were simply a polite compliment from a naturally chivalrous guy, for one tiny moment she almost believed him.

More than satisfied by his stunned reaction, she said, 'Don't sound so surprised,' and sashayed her way across the lounge room towards him.

He recovered enough to close his jaw, his blatant approval setting her pulse tripping as he toyed with his undone tie.

'I didn't plan on taking sticks with me tonight.'

'Pardon?'

'To beat off the guys who're going to be flocking around you,' he said, his hand stilling as she stopped in front of him. 'And you thought tonight would be boring.'

She laughed. 'It certainly won't be if you keep flattering me like that. I can't wait to see you beat off all those guys.'

'Just remember who you're coming home with,' he said, staring into her eyes, his expression surprisingly serious.

'I'll remember,' she murmured, knowing he was just stating a fact, hating the way her heart leapt in crazy expectation.

Breaking eye contact by sending a venomous look at the bow tie in his hands, he said, 'You wouldn't by any chance know how to fix one of these? It's been a long time since I've worn one and I can't seem to get the hang of it.'

'Here, let me,' she said, taking the scrap of black silk out of his hands, hoping her hands wouldn't shake as she slipped it around his neck, wishing he didn't smell so darn good.

She didn't go in for smelly aftershaves, hating the overpowering 'tickle up the nose' thing most of them gave her, but standing this close to Bo, enveloped in a subtle blend of spice and oak, she had to refrain from leaning forward and sniffing his neck like a basset-hound.

He stiffened when her fingers accidentally brushed the soft skin on the nape of his neck and she quickly finished the task, her fingers turning all thumbs as she tied the final knot.

'Thanks.'

He grimaced and stuck a finger between the stiff snowy-white collar of his dress shirt and his neck.

'Yet another thing I don't miss about working in finance every day.'

'Ties not your thing?'

He nodded. 'That, and the whole mundane routine of shower and shave every morning, getting trussed up to impress, being judged because of it.'

She could sympathise with him there. One of the joys of being self-employed and working from home was the freedom to bounce around make-up-less and to work in her underwear if she chose.

'So you didn't thrive in the cutthroat world of making money?'

'What do you think?'

His wry smile didn't soften his features. Instead, shadows swooped across his eyes before he banished them in a blink.

'I'll never forget the look on my dad's face the morning I walked into his office and told him I was giving up the lure of the almighty dollar for writing. It was priceless.'

'He approved though, right?'

Once again, darkness descended like a heavy cloak, his expression returning to its familiar gloom, and she silently cursed herself for spoiling the mood.

'Yeah, he did. It was Brennan who thought I was nuts, but we got through it. We're mates.'

Not good ones, if his sour expression was any indication.

Aiming to lighten the mood, she said, 'You're lucky. You're a talented guy to be able to make the switch from finance to author. I bet your dad and your brother buy every one of your books and pass it out to the CEOs at their corporate meetings.'

'You think?'

Bo's lips curved into a smile and she sent a high-five heavenward. Her plan to get the evening back on track had worked. Now, if she could keep her big mouth shut for the rest of the night, they might actually get through it without her annoying him or interrogating him or, worse, flirting with him.

'I'm sure of it,' she said, tapping her watch and jerking her head towards the door. 'Isn't it time we left?'

Running a hand through his artistically mussed hair, he said, 'Let's go.'

As Tahnee stepped through the door Bo held open for her, she couldn't help but wonder if tonight might be a good opportunity to get her boss to loosen up a bit. They'd got past the awkward post-kiss day, and for the last few minutes, had actually been able to hold a civil conversation.

Wouldn't it be so much easier if they could be friends over the next two weeks rather than nervous employee and broody boss?

Crossing her fingers as she tried not to fall flat on her face in previously untried three-inch heels, she followed him to the car, hoping tonight would be the start of a beautiful new friendship…and not the end of her dream if she rubbed him up the wrong way yet again.

'Who's the babe?'

Bo stiffened, turning in time to see a copy-editor jerking his head in Tahnee's direction as he spoke to an up-and-coming agent.

Annoyed at the guy's sleazy tone—and at himself for caring—he eavesdropped.

'Tahnee Lewis. Illustrator, I think,' the agent said, his gaze firmly fixed on Tahnee while the two guys grinned like adolescents.

'She's hot.'

The copy-editor's tongue was hanging out of his head and, for a second, Bo had visions of bustling Tahnee out of here like an overprotective jerk before taking a calming breath.

He'd brought her here. Hell, he'd practically ordered her to accompany him, yet, somehow, the evening wasn't quite turning out as he expected.

He'd hoped to make polite small talk with his publisher and their affiliates, maybe talk up his latest marketing strategy while Tahnee did what she did best: talk, bubble away, and bounce around the room like a hyperactive kid.

Well, he'd got that part right.

She knew how to work a room, that's for sure. He'd barely introduced her around when several publishers had whisked her away, plying her with drinks and goodness-knows-what promises of lucrative deals.

He should've been concerned, but strangely he wasn't. If she'd tolerated his grumpy behaviour for the last two days and hadn't fled yet, instinct told him she'd stick it out.

He knew her previous publisher had gone under—maybe she needed this job more than she let on?

Whatever, it was her business and, unlike his inquisitive illustrator, he had no desire to stick his nose where it didn't belong.

She glanced up at that precise moment, their gazes locking across the room and he tilted his head in her direction, acknowledging her cheeky quirked eyebrow. In response, she winked and turned back to the CEO of some publishing conglomerate, leaving him with a glorious view of her bare back.

For a guy who didn't do distractions, his lungs along with his brain had seized when he'd first seen her in that knockout dress.

Correction—seen her knockout body in that striking dress and by the tight band constricting his chest right now—not to mention the extreme tightness in his pants—his reaction to her hadn't dimmed.

If anything, watching her charm her way into some

old dude's graces added to her appeal; it took a lot of willpower to stand there and look rather than make a run for it and hole up in his mansion like he had for the last five years.

He didn't need this.

Apart from the mistake he'd made last night in trying to teach her a lesson, he'd been doing great in viewing her as just an employee.

Until he'd seen her in that dress, with her hair piled loosely on her head and subtle make-up highlighting her exquisite features, wearing her signature sassy smile and blue eyes gleaming in permanent amusement.

He'd known in that god-awful second that he was attracted to her despite every protest to the contrary. And the knowledge had been like an annoying bug biting his ass ever since.

He watched her as she bid a gracious farewell to the old codger, smiled and nodded to others in the group and made her way towards him, a confident smile on her face, a smile that knocked the breath out of him now that he'd been stupid enough to acknowledge the spark between them.

'You're not mingling much.'

'Too busy keeping an eye on you,' he said, grabbing two champagne flutes from a passing waiter and handing her one.

'Jealous?'

She raised a flute in his direction before taking a sip.

'Making sure you don't get too cosy with any of the opposition.'

In every sense of the word. He'd never been the jealous type, yet watching Tahnee with other men, hot on the heels of the shocking realisation he wanted her, had brought out the protective caveman in him. Now, if he could only haul her back to his cave without the hair pulling and chest beating.

'You know I'm yours till the end of next week,' she said, casting him a coy look from beneath lowered lashes, a look designed to tease, a look that could make a man crazy if he let it.

'Lucky me.'

Surprise widened her eyes, their unique blue colour offset perfectly by her shimmering dress.

'Be careful, boss. That almost sounded like flirting.'

He sent her a mock frown. 'Me, flirting? You must be mistaken.'

'You're too complex for me.'

She sipped her champagne, her gaze fixed on him over the rim of her glass as he wondered if this was such a good idea. If he'd lost his head once around her already, what hope did he have for restraint now that he'd admitted to an attraction between them?

'Actually, I'm a pretty simple guy.'

She rolled her eyes and lowered her glass. 'Yeah, as simple as a cryptic crossword.'

'In that case, how good are you at clues?'

'So-so. Why?'

'Unravel this,' he said, placing his hand in the small of her back like he'd been wanting to do all night, savouring the warm, smooth skin beneath his palm, lingering for a caressing touch for what seemed an eternity before he gently guided her to one side. 'I see my agent. Please excuse me for a moment. Perhaps you'll be ready to leave when I've finished?'

She stared at him in shock, her pupils dilated, her mouth a delectable, tempting rosebud.

Touching her wasn't the smartest thing he'd ever done and, as he strode across the crowded room, he had a sneaking suspicion he had a whole repertoire of even dumber moves to come.

Tahnee flew into the Ladies and collapsed onto a gilt-edged day bed.

This couldn't be happening.

She'd been psyching herself up all night to play the dutiful employee, to make contacts, to schmooze, to impress Bo into offering her an extension on her two-week contract if she was lucky.

And she'd been doing great till the last few minutes when her grumpy boss had done the biggest about-face of all time and actually flirted with her.

Not only that, he'd touched her!

Okay, so a light hand on the back to move her out of the way couldn't be construed as any great overture by any stretch of the imagination, but the minute his palm had touched her she'd lost all ability to think, let alone speak.

Heat, swift and scorching, had branded her back, sending fire racing through her body, fanning the flames of her imagination.

Could he be as attracted to her as she was to him?

And, if so, how far could this go?

How far could she push him before he reverted to stuffy old Bo, frowning at her whenever she so much as glanced his way?

She could try the direct approach: are you attracted to me? Too direct.

How about extending our deadline? Too corny.

Or the worst one: I've got a crush on you, so why don't we get creative together?

They all sucked big time.

To make matters worse, she hadn't handled the shock of his flirting well. Though at least she hadn't snorted the champagne out her nostrils or choked on it.

She needed time to absorb the fact that the guy she'd been secretly drooling over since she'd walked into his kitchen and seen that adorable crease between his brow might share a spark of interest in return. She needed time for her stomach to settle and stop with the internal cartwheels.

Crossing to the mirror, she fiddled with her hair and made sure her make-up still looked presentable, wishing she had some idea what to do. However, the longer she stared at her reflection, the more her tummy tumbled and spun, so she headed for the door.

She'd always faced things head-on, a trait learned as a feisty third-grader when she'd taken down the biggest bully at Stockton primary for taking a swipe at her foster parents.

Taking down a grouchy boss should be easy in comparison.

* * *

'When the hermit finally decides to leave the house, he goes all out, huh?'

Bo paused on the Opera House steps, sending her a glimmer of a smile. 'It doesn't happen very often, so now I'm out, better make the most of it. Don't you want to have a coffee after all?'

'Lead the way,' Tahnee said, waving her hand in a flourish towards the footpath leading to The Rocks, one of Sydney's oldest areas and the most beautifully restored. 'I might even push my luck and ask for a raise while you're in this uncharacteristic carefree mood.'

'Oh, yeah, heading to a café for a coffee is really taking a walk on the wild side.'

His wry grin seemed more relaxed than anything she'd seen yet. 'I might even go the whole hog and order a mud cake to go with it.'

'Ooh...a guy who likes to live dangerously. I like that.'

Their gazes locked and she blushed, cursing her loose tongue for blurting out the first thing that popped into her head. She'd virtually implied she liked him and that was more information than he needed to know.

'Bet you'll like the richest chocolate cake on the eastern seaboard of Australia more.'

I doubt that, she thought, knowing a mere dessert couldn't compare with the yummy treat before her, though this time she wisely kept her mouth shut.

She couldn't read him in this unpredictable mood, and though she wanted to push him a tad, to flirt and see where it led, she had a feeling she was playing with fire and could get burned.

After her mad dash to the Ladies, she'd returned in a jaunty mood and had proceeded to hassle him to leave, expecting him to head straight back to the mansion and revert to his cantankerous self.

Instead, he'd invited her to take a stroll down to The Rocks, one of her favourite parts of Sydney, and she'd accepted all too readily, hoping to make the most of this new, improved version of her grouchy boss.

'You're awfully quiet,' he said, stopping at the bottom of the steps and holding out a hand to help her down the last steps.

'I thought you'd be rapt by that,' she said, hesitating a fraction of a second before placing her hand in his and letting him guide her down the last few steps, her pulse accelerating at breakneck speed at the feel of his long, elegant fingers closing over hers.

'I suppose having you quiet rather than bombarding me with personal questions is unusual, and a rather welcome change.'

He didn't sound annoyed and she searched his face, trying to get a feel for his mood by reading his expression.

'What can I say? I love a good mystery and you're so tight-lipped, I can't help myself.'

To her surprise, his eyes glittered with amusement rather than the usual coldness she'd come to expect when she presented him with her blunt honesty.

'Tight-lipped, huh?'

'Very!'

'Well, we'll just have to remedy that, won't we?'

Before she could ask how, his mouth swooped down to capture hers, shattering her with the hunger of his kiss.

She couldn't think. She couldn't move.

Every cell in her body leapt to life, craving more as he deepened the kiss, his lips teasing her to match him, to challenge him, to give, as well as receive.

She felt her knees wobble as his mouth repeatedly grazed hers, brushing her lips with agonising control when all she craved was for him to devour her.

Her body ignited and her emotions whirled out of control as she clung to him, helpless to fight the onslaught of sensation short-circuiting her brain. As he slowly pulled away, her lips burned in the aftermath of the most explosive kiss she'd ever experienced.

'I thought we weren't supposed to do that any more?'

She stared up at him, the kiss leaving her weak-kneed and more confused than ever.

'We weren't,' he said, his voice cold and flat, totally at odds with the fire burning in his eyes.

'You afraid someone might see the great Bo Bradford snogging in public?'

'Do I look afraid?'

No, he looked mad, angrier than she'd ever seen him—considering his foul mood most of the time, that was saying something.

Taking a deep breath, she made an instantaneous decision to tackle him head-on. If she was going to get any work done for the rest of the two weeks, she needed answers, starting now.

'Don't you dare go all stuffy and self-righteous on me now.'

She jabbed a finger in his direction, stopping short of touching that fabulous hard chest she'd copped an all-too-brief feel of during that scintillating kiss.

'You keep trying to push me away with that crabby manner of yours, but I know you want me.'

Oops! She hadn't quite meant to put it like that, but once the words had slipped out, she was somewhat grateful. Let's see Mr Reclusive get himself out of this one.

Reaching for her, he gripped her upper arms, his fingers clamping on to her skin and flooding her body with fluid heat.

'What do you want me to say? That you're wrong? That you're crazy? That I don't want you? Fine, I'll say it.'

'Liar,' she murmured, moistening her bottom lip with the tip of her tongue, enjoying the way his eyes flickered there, glowing with suppressed desire.

Sighing, he slowly raised his gaze to hers, banked heat blazing like a roaring inferno. 'This is not supposed to happen. I don't want this to happen.'

'What? It's only a kiss.'

Yeah, right, and she was just drawing pictures for a hobby.

'That's bull and we both know it.'

His fingers slid down her arms, creating a soft trail of tingles that wouldn't quit when he reached her hands and held on to them tight. 'I don't need complications in my life. I have my career and that's all that matters.'

'And?'

She had a feeling he was leading up to something. If he would only get to the point before she burst.

'I can't get you out of my mind. Ever since you walked in the door you've been a distraction and tonight in that dress…'

His gaze skimmed over her, lingering in all the right places as blood pounded through her body. 'I know this is crazy. I know this goes against everything I've said before, but I want you. And by the way you've responded to my kisses, I'd say you want me, too. We've got less than two weeks—how about we make the most of it?'

Her heart thudded and flipped over as his words sank in. Bo wanted her and she should be thrilled. Yet 'making the most' of their time together could mean a lot of things and she needed it spelled out before she jumped to any way-out conclusions, another character flaw along with her perpetual nosiness—or so Nina liked to point out.

'What are you suggesting?'

'Perhaps we set down a few ground rules?'

'Such as?'

'We strictly adhere to keep things platonic during work hours.'

She was dying to ask him to clarify what happened out of work hours, but she'd go along with him for now. If she gave him enough rope, he might create a great big noose without any help from her.

'So what constitutes work hours?'

'Nine to five?'

'Uh-huh. And what are the other ground rules?'

His eyes never left hers; for all his cool, calculated control, he could've been presenting a well-constructed synopsis to his editor rather than asking her to do what she thought he was.

'Whatever happens out of work hours doesn't affect our working relationship, not now, not later.'

Tugging her hands free of his, she held up two fingers.

'So rule two is we keep things light? No heavy expectations on either side?'

He nodded and she balled her other hand into a tight fist. Was he for real? He was outlining the dream arrangement for every guy on the planet: stress-free, fun sex with no commitment—and he expected her to go for it?

Holding her temper in check, just, she raised a third finger. 'Come on, I bet you're saving the best for last.'

'Rule three, this all ends in a fortnight.'

Tahnee stared at Bo, as stunned by his cocky proposal as his swift turnaround from testy boss to hot-to-trot.

She should've slapped him and told him what he could do with his damn rules.

Instead, 'done' teetered on the edge of her tongue rather than 'shove it.'

What if this spark they shared was unique?

What if, once they got started up, they couldn't stop?

She'd never been a believer in fate, but something about the intensity of their attraction, their connection on so many levels from professional to intellectual and beyond, had her wondering 'what if?'

What if there was more than a physical attraction here?

What if they were sensational together?

What if he wanted more than two weeks?

'What if two weeks with me aren't enough?'

She tried to make light of it, hoping to get a laugh out of him when, in fact, she hung on his answer.

He smiled, but it wasn't the sexy, carefree smile she'd hoped for. Instead, it held a hint of sadness and she wondered why—or who—had made such a cynic out of a guy who had the world at his feet yet shunned it.

'It will be.'

He didn't mince words, just as she'd expected and she shook her head, knowing she had to tread carefully if she didn't want to blow her dream job right here, right now, all for the chance to knock Bo off his incredible high horse.

'Thanks, but no thanks.'

She glanced at her watch, faked a yawn and shifted her weight from side to side. 'I'd really like to head back now rather than have a coffee. It's been quite a night.'

'I've offended you.'

He reached out for her and she edged away, not wanting to give her traitorous body an opportunity to overturn the logical decisions made by her head.

'You've surprised me,' she corrected, knowing it would be hypocritical of her to be totally horrified by his proposal.

Hadn't she wanted to push him? To flirt with him? To make him see her as a desirable woman rather than a mere employee?

Well, she'd got her wish…and how!

He opened his mouth as if to say something else and she held up a hand to stave it off.

'Let's drop it. I'm tired. I want to head back, okay?'

He stared at her, embarrassment and regret mingling in his eyes, and she turned away and headed for the car.

It was going to be a long two weeks.

CHAPTER SEVEN

Wally didn't like water. He felt big and slow and couldn't swim well. But the watering hole was the quietest spot in the morning and Kaz didn't come down there. He liked having a new friend to help him with his work but he didn't like the funny looks she gave him. As for blowing kisses like she had last night…yuck!
Bo Bradford's blog. Wednesday morning.

TAHNEE bounced out of bed after a surprisingly good night's sleep. No hot dreams of Bo—despite his outlandish proposal last night—no dreams period, a surprise in itself, considering she often dreamt of her foster family. Always the same dream—she'd be in the kitchen helping Doris make apple pie and Stan would be sitting at the table, reading his newspaper with a mock frown while secretly smiling at her antics.

The childless couple who'd lived in Stockton their entire lives had been great parents: supportive yet strict, encouraging yet firm, with an abundance of love that came straight from their big hearts. They'd welcomed her into their home and treated her like the daughter they had never had and she wasn't surprised that even now, seven years after their death, she still dreamt about the warmth they'd created as a family.

She missed it; missed the comfort of belonging, of sharing, of knowing there was another person in the house at night. When Doris and Stan had died within six months of each other—Doris of an aneurysm, Stan of diabetic complications—she'd been devastated, though in a way losing them had been the catalyst for her to find her sisters.

'Good things always come out of bad,' Doris would say and Tahnee had clung to that motto throughout the long search for her sisters. Thankfully, Doris had been right. Being reunited with Carissa and Kristen had been all good, yet a small part of her still yearned for the cosy cottage with its picket fence, warm kitchen and loving couple to fill it.

Padding across the bedroom, Tahnee pulled up the Roman blinds and blinked several times. Not from the morning sun streaming through the wide windows, but from the dazzling sight greeting her: Bo, almost naked barring a par of funky red-and-black board-shorts, the kind surfers wore, standing on the edge of the pool twenty metres away, poised to dive into the crystal-clear water.

If her mouth wasn't dry from the morning-after effects of the few glasses of champagne she'd had last night, it certainly would be now as she stared, her gaze riveted as he swam a lazy four laps of the Olympic size pool before hoisting himself out and reaching for a towel.

However, in the time it took him to reach for the towel, about thirty glorious seconds, she had an unimpeded view of a bronzed, muscular body covered in beading water droplets. Thirty fantastic, illicit seconds where she could ogle his broad chest covered in a light smattering of dark hair, moving lower to his firm abs, and lower to his—

'Ouch!'

Her head snapped back as she bumped her forehead on the glass. That'd teach her for leaning so far forward for a better look.

Unfortunately, her rather clumsy head-clunking blew her cover as Bo glanced up and mistook her rubbing her sore forehead for a wave and waved back.

Great, now he'd think she'd been perving on him, which she had, of course, but he didn't have to know about it.

Ready to bolt into the shower, she took a step back and caught her little toe on the corner of an armchair.

'Sh-eesh!' she cried out, collapsing into the chair and grabbing at her toe, sore forehead momentarily forgotten.

Her little pinkie throbbed, her pride smarted and then she had to go and look out the window…only to find the cause of her pain grinning.

'It's not bloody funny,' she mumbled, knowing her deadly glare would be lost at this range, and, muttering curses that a lady shouldn't know, hobbled to the bathroom without a backward glance.

'Breakfast?'

Tahnee strolled into the kitchen as if she didn't have

a care in the world, ignoring the constant ache in her toe, which had subsided slightly once she'd traded her favourite red boots for pink beaded flip-flops. Another bonus of her denim fetish: jeans looked great with any footwear.

'Just coffee, thanks,' she said, heading for the espresso machine.

'Sure? I whip up a mean omelette.'

She hadn't risked a glance Bo's way yet, but something in his voice told her she wouldn't be able to avoid him for long.

'After all, you can't take painkillers on an empty stomach.'

He was laughing at her. That 'something' in his voice was out-and-out amusement.

What had happened to him? She'd expected him to revert to type today, turning all sulky after their cold silence on the drive home last night and the frigidly polite goodnight. Instead, here he was, commenting on her clumsiness, alluding to her perving on him and laughing at her to boot.

'You're a real riot,' she said, folding her arms and leaning against the bench, surreptitiously lifting her foot with the offending toe while mustering the fiercest glare she could.

His lips curved into a delicious smile, the type of smile that could melt a girl's heart if she weren't in pain—or determined to ignore him for his cool, calculated way of presenting what could be the most fun she'd had in ages—but she was, so he could take his smile and shove it.

'You okay?'

'No.' She glared, he smiled and her resistance wavered.

'Want me to take a look at it? Make sure it's not broken?'

'No.'

His voice dropped lower, the gentle coaxing tone sending the last of her resistance up in smoke. 'You know, maybe if you let me look at it, I could rub it for you. A good massage might help.'

'No!'

The last thing she needed was his hands anywhere near her, even an innocuous appendage like a toe.

Softening her voice, she said, 'It's not my ankle or my foot, it's my toe. I stubbed it, no big deal. But thanks for the offer.'

'Suit yourself,' he said, sliding into a seat and piling his plate with toast. 'Your loss. I give a great massage.'

Tahnee gulped and turned away, concentrating on her coffee rather than the thought of Bo's hands on her...all over her...stroking...

'You could've joined me.'

Blinking away her erotic thoughts, she took her coffee and joined him at the table.

'I'm not a morning person. Swimming is the last thing I'd want to do first thing.'

His gaze locked on hers and, for some unfathomable reason, she blushed.

She never blushed. She gave cheek, she gave smart comebacks, she never blushed, but something about the way Bo looked at her, as if he knew exactly what she'd rather do first thing in the morning—with him—had heat surging into her cheeks.

'I'm sorry, by the way.' He broke the tension by slathering butter and thick apricot jam on a piece of toast, and peanut butter on another.

'For what?'

She took a tentative sip of her steaming coffee, not liking the teasing quirk of his lips. He'd already apologised for his outlandish proposal last night and, right now, he didn't look sorry for anything. In fact, he looked like a guy about to slam her with another one-liner.

'For being such a distraction.'

He took a big bite of toast, chewed and swallowed while she ignored what he was implying. Until he went that one step further, of course.

'I must've looked pretty impressive out there for you to risk concussion and a broken toe just to sneak a peek.'

She spluttered, the coffee catching in her throat as she reached for a napkin—not to dab her mess, but to wad into a ball and throw at his big head.

He laughed as her throw went wide, taunting her further by offering the stack of napkins to have another shot.

'You're so not worth it,' she said, cradling her mug in both hands and wishing it offered more of a defence against his smug smile and sparkling eyes.

'That's not what you thought half an hour ago.'

Another annoying crunch of toast while his eyes teased and challenged and begged her to fire back.

She'd said she wouldn't do this.

Last night, her mind had been made up as she'd mulled over how to handle this on the way home. Her decision? No trading quips, no flirting, no funny stuff.

But he wasn't playing fair—what was a girl to do?

'I wasn't perving on you. You just happened to be in my line of vision when I opened the blinds.'

'Uh-huh.'

His grunted response said he didn't believe her for a second.

She tried another tack.

'Besides, you weren't that impressive. I was checking out the view of the harbour beyond the pool. It's spectacular.'

Totally accurate, but, truth be told, her gaze hadn't quite made it to the harbour this morning—it had been riveted to Bo's body.

'Hmm.'

Damn him, he still didn't believe her.

'Even if I was looking at you for just a second, the sight of you in shorts wouldn't send me crazy or anything. I just tripped, that's all…' she finished lamely, her mouth twitching with barely suppressed laughter as he gave her his best solemn nod.

'Stop it. You're not helping,' she said, draining her coffee and slamming the mug down on the table.

'Helping what?'

He leaned forward, his hand bringing the toast to his mouth poised mid-lift.

My anti-Bo policy.

Her new, stay-professional-at-all-costs image, the

new and improved Tahnee, the girl who didn't fall for guys she'd known for less than a week, especially guys who wanted to have their cake and eat it, too.

'Forget it,' she said, pushing back from the table and heading for the door, wincing when she inadvertently put extra weight on her toe. 'I'm going to work.'

His chuckles followed her out the door.

'I brought you something.'

Tahnee hadn't looked up at him when he'd entered the office; by the set of her jaw, she was purposely ignoring him.

No problems, considering it gave him all the time in the world to study her: blond hair caught up in some weird clip complete with pink feather, long eyelashes shading eyes the colour of Sydney Harbour on a cloudless summer day and sensuous lips with just a hint of gloss.

Lips he'd tasted, lips that had haunted his dreams last night, lips which taunted him to come back for seconds and thirds.

Now that he'd made it clear he was attracted to her, he could stand here all day and watch her, admiring the curve of her breasts outlined clearly in another tight T-shirt, pale blue today, and her long legs encased in faded denim.

She was the whole package, from the tips of her layered hair to her pinkie toe, which, even at this distance, he could see had swelled to almost double its size.

Suddenly struck by how painful the toe looked, he stepped forward and held out the icepack he'd brought when hit by a pang of conscience after she'd stalked/hobbled from the kitchen.

'Put this on your toe. It'll help with the swelling.'

She glanced up and, rather than glimpsing annoyance as he'd expected, surprised him yet again with a genuine teasing sparkle in her eyes.

'Is this your idea of a peace offering? A lousy pack of frozen peas wrapped in a dishcloth?'

He shrugged and made to turn away. 'Fine, if you don't want it—'

'Thanks, I'll take it.'

She made a frantic grab at the icepack, which told him exactly how much pain she must be in.

'You should've told me it was this bad.'

He sat next to her, picked up her foot and placed it on a cushion with icepack *in situ*.

'You would've laughed at me anyway.'

She winced as he readjusted the pack, biting down on her bottom lip, and he felt like a heel for laughing off her pain earlier.

'You sure it's not broken?'

She shook her head, setting aside her sketchpad and charcoals and regarding him with an intensity that had him squirming. 'No, because I've broken it before. This is just a bad stub. I'll live, which is more than I can say for you.'

'What did I do?'

Her stare wavered and, for a second, he glimpsed vulnerability in her eyes. 'Last night. The whole kiss thing and your stupid ground rules.'

He aimed for levity, not knowing where this was

going and hoping he wouldn't find out. 'You're going to kill me over one kiss? I'd hate to see what would happen if we went the whole way.'

To his amazement, she blushed. Super-confident women with smart mouths like her didn't blush. Then again, he'd been out of circulation for a while—maybe things had changed.

She sighed, an exasperated sound indicating she didn't appreciate his humour.

'I know I wanted to kill you last night, but I've been thinking. I've been teasing you a fair bit, trying to get you to loosen up, so I don't blame you entirely for wanting the fling thing.'

'The fling thing?'

He tried to keep a straight face, but his lips twitched the harder he tried to fight it.

'See! That's exactly what I mean.' She jabbed towards his mouth. 'You didn't do that when I first arrived. In fact, you've been the stuffiest, most uptight guy I've ever met. But since last night you've been smiling and teasing and laughing and it's too hard.'

'Too hard?'

She didn't know the half of it!

'Keeping things platonic. Not flirting, not kissing, and the rest.'

She paused, her mouth softening, and it took all his willpower not to lean across the couch, haul her into his arms and do exactly what she didn't want him to do. 'What made you do a Jekyll and Hyde, anyway?'

He'd been contemplating the very same question all

night, since sleep had eluded him. Several reasons had sprung to mind, most of them involving his reclusive lifestyle, but he'd known they were a crock. Quite simply, Tahnee had wrought a change almost without him knowing and it felt good. It felt downright fantastic. Why shouldn't he have a little fun with a beautiful woman for the first time in ages?

He worked hard enough.

He deserved it.

And it wasn't like anyone would discover his secret because of it.

'Honestly?'

She pinned him with an astute stare. 'It's the only way to be.'

Maybe he was making a huge mistake in opening up to her? Maybe it would be inviting trouble just when his world had finally righted itself?

Suddenly, he didn't care.

He and his pal Wally had been holed up by themselves for far too long. If Wally could let Kaz into his life, he could take a chance on Tahnee.

'Honestly? I've been living like a hermit for too long. My work is my focus. I've dated occasionally, done the obligatory socialising with work colleagues at publishing functions, but other than that I've deliberately kept to myself. Moira was unobtrusive and work stayed work. Then you came along, and in less than a few days I'm thinking along very unprofessional lines.'

'Oh.'

One, short syllable uttered on a soft breath as she sank back against the cushions, looking decidedly sheepish.

'That honest enough for you?'

Sure was for him. Saying out loud what he'd been thinking all night felt like a weight had rolled off his shoulders. Work had always been enough for him, the imaginary world of his characters so much more appealing than the crazy world he lived in. Yet something had changed last night the minute he'd seen Tahnee in that dress; suddenly, he'd known he couldn't go back to hiding behind his work, no matter how much he wanted to.

'Well, aren't you going to say anything? Guys aren't used to opening up like that and here I am, feeling kinda uncertain—the least you can do is reassure me.'

Her cheeky smile kicked in at that. 'You don't need reassurance. I think you got all the reassurance you need when I responded to your kiss last night.'

'It was pretty spectacular, wasn't it?'

'Too right.'

They stared at each other, the same sexual tension from yesterday stretching taut between them; as her lips parted in a tiny *O,* the blood from his brain rushed south.

'You know those unprofessional thoughts I mentioned a second ago?'

'Yeah?'

She leaned forward a fraction and he wondered if she knew what an appealing picture she presented: beautiful, eager, wanting.

'I'm having some of them right now.'

She smiled, a coy curving of her lips designed to tease, to tantalise.

'Maybe I was being a bit harsh in telling you to shove your offer.'

'Maybe,' he said, unable to keep his hands off her a minute longer, resting his hand on her ankle and tracing slow circles around her jutting bones with his thumb.

She shuddered, a blissful expression illuminating her face as she stared at his hand, mesmerised.

'Perhaps I should amend it?'

'Perhaps.'

He increased the pressure, sliding his hand downward to cup her foot, his thumb working on her instep now.

Her eyelids fluttered shut for a brief moment and he smiled, enjoying her obvious pleasure at his touch. If she liked his foot massages, wait till he started on the rest of her. Not that he was cocky, but something had shifted between them in the last few minutes, a barrier between them had come down.

Suddenly, her eyes flew open and she fixed him with that open stare only she did so well.

'I need to finish drawing this scene, otherwise we'll never make deadline. Thanks for the massage.'

She all but jerked her foot out of his hand, leaving him no option but to replace it gently on the cushion, refasten the icepack and head for his desk.

'I guess I should be applauding your work ethic,' he said, sitting down and glancing at his inbox with little interest, wishing he still held her delicate foot in his hand. Pathetic, but he'd take whatever physical contact he could get at this point.

'Don't applaud me yet. You haven't seen the finished result of the second-last chapter.'

As if to prove a point, she propped her sketchpad vertically on her lap, effectively screening him out.

'I trust you,' he said, opening the last chapter he'd been working on, wondering if he'd be able to get anything done now his libido had been hotwired into action and all he could focus on was the luscious woman sitting on the couch opposite.

He trusted her.

It was himself he was having trouble trusting.

Tahnee didn't know whether to be insulted or flattered by Bo's attention. Now that he'd gone all nice and normal on her, she almost wished he'd revert to cold and stuffy.

That guy she could handle. This new, improved version of Bo was driving her out of her mind.

She shouldn't even contemplate what he'd suggested last night, but the longer she sat here with the tension between them stretched to breaking point, she knew that her initial holier-than-thou response might not have been the most honest.

So what if she had a wild, passionate fling with Bo and it ended in two weeks? She'd be bored, let down, single—three things she was right now without the promise of sizzling sex thrown in.

For she had no doubt the sex would be amazing. If he kissed like a dream, he'd have all the moves down pat. Not to mention he didn't get out much; if he hadn't had sex in a while, well… Her cheeks heated at the thought, not to mention the throb of her own nether regions, which hadn't seen much action in a long time.

Nibbling her bottom lip, she drew a pouch on Wally rather than Kaz, scrubbing furiously when she realised her mistake.

How could she focus on drawing cute animals when Bo sat behind his desk, like a sexy, ruffled, eccentric magnet? She couldn't keep her eyes off him.

Ironic that she'd wanted to draw him out of his shell, tease him a little, get him to notice her. After last night, he'd come out of his shell well and truly, smashing it to smithereens along the way.

'What's up?'

He looked up from his PC screen and she dropped her gaze, but not quickly enough if his smug grin was any indication.

Damn him, he knew she'd been staring.

'Nothing, just trying to get a grumpy expression for Wally and thought you'd be good inspiration for that.'

He sat back, folded his hands and placed them behind his head, his cocky posture serving to accentuate his broad chest, the soft cotton of his black T-shirt pulled taut across it.

'But I'm not grumpy any more, remember? You've seen to that.'

She let out an exasperated huff, determinedly staring at her sketchpad rather than his smirk.

She'd always used a smart mouth and quick wit to get the upper hand in any situation. It had served her well, the perfect self-protective mechanism to hide her vulnerability at not fitting in or not belonging. In the early years she'd done anything and everything to please Doris and Stan, taking a long time to learn she didn't have to as they loved her unconditionally anyway, but she'd never been able to shake the habit.

Of course, it went a long way to explaining why she hadn't shut up since she'd walked through Bo's door.

Yet now her quick wit had deserted her, along with every ounce of common sense she'd ever possessed if the persistent throbbing in her body the moment he so much as glanced her way was any indication.

'No comeback?'

She ignored his taunt. 'No time. Must work.'

'Okay,' he said, his low chuckles washing over her, teasing her to look up, to join in whatever game he was playing.

Ignoring the urge to look up, she fixed on her sketches till her eyes blurred.

She could switch off her mind, ignore her instincts and try to concentrate on work. Or she could get real and face facts.

She was attracted to Bo.

More attracted than she'd ever been to any other guy before.

She could play the outraged virgin for the remainder of her time here.

Or she could have the wildest fling of her life.

The choice was hers and her gut churned with a potent mixture of anticipation and dread: anticipation of what having a fling with a spectacular guy like Bo would be like, dread at the consequences.

As much as she'd like to make out she could handle a fling, it wasn't her style. Never had been, never would be.

Every guy she'd been out with had been sized up for F potential: future, father, fun and for ever. Not that she expected Bo to live up to anything but the fun part of her F equation, but what if she added another F to the list in the form of fool?

For-ever type of girls always ended up feeling like fools when they hoped for futures that weren't there or could never be. Hopefully, she'd be too busy concentrating on the fun part to worry about the rest.

Sighing, she laid down her charcoal and flexed her toes gingerly, pleased when pain didn't shoot up her foot.

She had to get out of here right now, before she let her gut rule her head, threw caution to the wind and accepted Bo's crazy offer.

'I'll see you later,' she said, not looking in his direction as she hobbled for the door.

'What happened to work?'

'Screw it,' she muttered, hating her word-association skills and the images it conjured up.

'Let me know if you need anything,' he said, his tone low and cajoling and she bolted from the room—well, made a lame attempt at bolting, considering her toe—wishing his soft chuckles didn't have the same reaction on her insides as his sensuous touch.

CHAPTER EIGHT

Wally had never felt so out of sorts. He usually spent most of his day digging in the dirt, but not today. Kaz had chatted a lot and, to Wally's surprise, he liked it. In fact, he liked Kaz. His tummy didn't feel so funny when she stared at him now and he even looked forward to later when she might blow him another good-night kiss.
Bo Bradford's blog, Wednesday afternoon.

TAHNEE had never been a clock-watcher.

She worked her own hours, eating when she felt hungry, taking a break when she needed to. Never in all her working years had she experienced anything like this intense compulsion to check her watch every five minutes, silently cursing when the hands didn't move fast enough for her liking.

It was all *his* fault.

She propped up her sketchbook, using it as an effective screen to check out the object of her discontent. For a savvy career girl, she'd let her brains turn to mush and all because of her stupid hormones.

Was she actually considering accepting his crazy ground rules and having a fling with her sexy boss?

She must be nuts.

Maybe all the years of drawing fictional characters had sucked her into believing she was one. But which one?

She couldn't be Cinderella; the long-dressed one had been too naïve, falling for the whole Prince Charming routine when Tahnee knew there was no such thing.

She couldn't be Sleeping Beauty; no way would she let any strange dude near her when she was sleeping, let alone allow him to kiss her.

Perhaps Little Red Riding Hood was more her style; bright clothes, a basket full of goodies, and a fear/fascination for the Big Bad Wolf.

Speaking of which, her big bad wolf had his brow furrowed as he stared at the computer screen, his fingers flying over the keyboard. At least one of them had no problem concentrating on work.

'Something wrong?'

She jumped. Somehow, he'd sensed her stare without looking up. So much for subtlety.

'No, just thinking.'

His fingers stopped clattering and he looked up, a knowing gleam in his eyes.

'Thought I could hear the wheels turning from here. Thinking about anything in particular?'

She racked her brain for a quick excuse and made a

mental grab for the first thought which popped into her head. 'Fairy tales.'

He pushed back from the desk, folded his arms and fixed her with an amused stare which read 'this is going to be good.'

'You're thinking about fairy tales?'

'Uh-huh, just likening what you write to fairy tales, that sort of thing,' she said, inordinately pleased with her quick save.

'Wally's more a realistic type of guy. He doesn't always have a happy ending.'

'Yeah, but the concept is basically the same. You bring joy to kids by inventing happy stories. Fairy tales do that, too.'

She sounded so plausible, he'd never know she'd been casting him in the role of a baddie about to rip off her cape rather than pondering the likeness of his writing to the Brothers Grimm.

'I'm looking forward to knock-off time, too,' he said, grinning at her like someone who had his cake and was about to eat it, too—in one huge gorging feast.

'What?'

'You tug at your right ear when you're fibbing, so I guessed your mind isn't on my stories and more along the lines of what we discussed over lunch. About you taking me to your favourite spot in Sydney for dinner?'

Tahnee dropped her right arm in record time, unaware she'd been fiddling with her earring, and sent him her best haughty glare. 'Perhaps you'd like me to add mind-reader to the list of your attributes, right alongside massive ego?'

His grin widened. 'You've made a list?'

Making an unladylike sound somewhere between a snort and a curse, she rattled the pages of her sketchbook in his general direction. Getting out of the house had seemed like a good idea at the time, out into public, but suddenly the idea of dinner for two held even more potential for intimacy than staying in. What had she been thinking to even suggest it?

'I'm going back to work. I suggest you do the same.'

Silence greeted her snooty proclamation. Surprising, since he always had to have the last word.

'You're right. Concentrating on work will make time fly and we both know how much we want five o'clock to roll around.'

Tahnee kept her eyes trained on a cute pic of Kaz and Wally sparring, knowing she should just ignore him, but unable to do so.

'Dream on.'

'Oh, I've been doing plenty of that and now I'm looking forward to the real thing.'

His silky tone taunted her, begged her to respond, to match wits with him, and a small part of her loved it. She admired a guy's bod like the next woman, but give her a glimpse of well-rounded intellect combined with a killer sense of humour and she was a goner.

Sighing, she finally looked up, aware that staring at him was infinitely more interesting than her drawings—

the same drawings she'd been staring at for the last fifteen minutes in an effort not to look at him.

'For a grumpy recluse, you've turned into Casanova pretty darn quick.'

His slow, sexy smile kicked her pulse into double time and she forced herself to stay seated rather than drape herself over his desk like she wanted.

'Thanks for elevating me to legendary-lover status. You must have a lot of faith.'

'Faith, stupidity, they're close relations.'

Any other guy would've wilted under her 'I don't give a damn' tone and stare.

But then, Bo wasn't just any other guy, which is why she needed a cold shower, a lobotomy or a combination of both.

'You know I'm teasing, right? I like to get a rise out of you.'

And I'd like to get a rise out of you.

Oh-oh, looked like her inner floozie needed that cold shower real quick.

'And you know I have no expectations, right?'

As if.

Guys always expected more, usually more than she was willing to give. She'd had no trouble fending off unwanted advances in the past, yet now she had a feeling she'd be doing more of the advancing.

'So you're telling me you don't want more than that kiss at the Opera House?'

He held out his hands as if showing her he had no tricks up his sleeves. 'No expectations, see? No preconceptions, no assumptions, just a vain hope you'll take pity on a guy who doesn't get out much and maybe ravish me one night in my sleep?'

Laughter bubbled out and she shook her head.

She didn't stand a chance against this guy. He'd crumbled her defences quicker than she could erect them.

'You never know your luck,' she said, wondering if he felt the same sense of impending inevitability hanging over them, the sense that, no matter what they said or how much they danced around each other, they'd end up having sex anyway.

'On that note, I'm going for a run.'

He stood, giving her a perfect view of the body she'd been ogling every second she could. She hated exercise, but if swimming and jogging could produce those sorts of results, he was a great advertisement to get off the couch.

'To burn off all the excess energy I've got.'

She registered his meaning, but didn't acknowledge it. Suddenly, her head ached from all the witty repartee and the sooner he removed his hot bod and sharp mind, the better.

'Have fun.'

She waved and pretended to add a few flourishes to her sketch, knowing she wouldn't do another skerrick of work once he left. Instead, she had a date with a razor, exfoliator and moisturiser, just in case.

'We will.'

She thought she'd imagined his murmured response laden with promise until she glanced up and caught his meaningful glance before he strolled out the door.

* * *

'Not tonight, dear, I have a headache,' Tahnee muttered at her reflection, grinning at the hypocrisy of her statement.

The only reason she had a headache was because she'd spent too long dithering over her wardrobe, followed by an inordinately long time in front of the mirror trying to achieve a no make-up look with make-up. She rarely bothered with the stuff back home, hence her extended stay at the mirror trying to curl lashes, prime for foundation and shade cheekbones.

As for 'not tonight,' she'd already made up her mind on that score. She was sticking to the fun part of her F motto, whatever that might entail.

Smacking her lips together after applying a sheer layer of gloss, she reached for the hairdryer in another first. She never, ever, blow-dried her hair, preferring to let it dry naturally. The only time she had silky smooth hair was after a visit to the hairdresser where they did the job for her. She was a low-maintenance kind of gal and preferred it that way, which explained her clueless state now as she tussled with hot, blasting air and a round spiked hairbrush.

After five angst-filled minutes and several close calls with burnt strands and frizz-control serum that obviously didn't deliver what it promised, she laid the hairdryer down in defeat and gathered her hair up in a high ponytail. Not the most seductive of looks, but hey, she'd gone way past her tolerance limit with the eyelash curler anyway.

Her mobile rang and she knew Nina must've used every ounce of her limited will power supply to wait this long to ring for an update following their texting session last night.

Checking the call display, Tahnee grinned and hit the answer button.

'Hey, Nina. What, no snazzy SMS tonight?'

'Can it, T., and tell me everything.'

Tahnee plopped onto the bed and propped her feet up, her grin widening as she caught sight of her pinkie toe, which had finally returned to normal proportions, recalling how she'd injured it in the first place.

'Firstly, how are the kids? I miss the munchkins.'

Nina sighed and Tahnee knew she'd be torn. Her friend loved Marian and Callum more than life itself and usually could spend hours talking about their latest achievements from mastering maths to pooing in the potty. But she loved a good gossip session, too, and right now she'd want to get down to the good stuff.

'Marian's fine. She's spelling champion of the second grade as of today and Callum is moving from potty to toilet. And, before you ask, Karl's fine, too. Now, spill it.'

Smoothing an imaginary crease from her denim skirt—another attempt to dress things up tonight, as she never wore skirts and had only brought this one after incessant nagging from Nina—she answered in her best naïve voice.

'The job's great. I'm illustrating two new characters for the latest book, which is due real soon and—'

'T.! Don't make me drive down there.'

Tahnee laughed. She wouldn't put anything past Nina and her quest for gossip.

'Okay, okay. I was going to call you earlier anyway, but got tied up getting ready for dinner.'

Nina's tone lowered a whole octave, the same tone she used on the kids to threaten—she called it persuading—them into doing something they didn't want to do.

'Dinner, sweetie? With anyone special?'

'If you call my boss special. Personally, I'd call him a big pain in the butt, but hey, that's just me.'

Tahnee knew she'd pushed Nina to the limit and waited for the fallout. She never tired of winding her up.

'Tahnee Lewis! If you don't tell me what's going on right this instant, I'll set Daisy on you.'

Tahnee chuckled, knowing Daisy, Stockton's octogenarian resident matchmaker, would have a field day with her and Bo. After all, look at the interference she'd run on Nina and Karl, all but pushing the two of them together, not to mention her sister Carissa and her husband Brody.

'Okay, you got me. You want the goss? Here it is. Bo is drop-dead gorgeous with a hot bod and fabulous smile. He has a great sense of humour and can match my comebacks, but the best bit—he gives great foot massages.'

Silence greeted her for all of two seconds before Nina squealed. 'You've known the guy less than a week and he's already touched your feet? Wow, T. You're a fast mover.'

'Don't worry, that's all he's touched.'

Though not for much longer if she had any say in it. 'He's a decent guy and I'm enjoying working with him. He was super grumpy to begin with, but has loosened up a lot.' Understatement of the year. 'It's a bonus that he's easy on the eye and can lighten up when needed.'

'Oh-oh.'

'What?'

'You never sing a guy's praises. You always talk down your dates.'

'And your point?'

Nina paused, obviously choosing her words very carefully. 'You must think this guy is pretty special to talk him up like that, especially to me.'

'Maybe he is.'

She spoke softly, opting for the truth as always. She might be many things—flighty, vivacious with a hankering for gossip—but she knew she wouldn't be contemplating having a fling with Bo unless she liked him. A lot.

Besides, if she couldn't confide in her best friend, she'd go nuts.

'Wow.'

Another pause, a shorter one this time before Nina rushed on. 'I'm happy for you. Enjoy yourself, have fun with this guy, but just be careful, okay?'

'Careful's my middle name,' she said, as they both guffawed.

A knock sounded on her bedroom door and she bolted upright, almost knocking her head on the lamp. Jeez, she'd end up with a serious injury by the end of the fortnight at this rate.

'Is that him?'

Tahnee smoothed down her skirt and slipped into flat

sandals, her favourite black ones with the gold, turquoise and emerald embroidery. 'Uh-huh.'

'At the risk of sounding like a prudish old maid, why is he knocking on your bedroom door?'

Tahnee smiled, opened the door and held up a finger to Bo, asking for a minute.

'How do you know I'm in my bedroom?'

Nina blew an exasperated sound, another standard weapon from her 'watch out, kids, I'm on the warpath' arsenal.

'Ask Marian and Callum. I have eyes in the back of my head, remember? A radar that extends all the way to Sydney.'

'Bye, Nina.'

'Bye. Love you. And be careful.'

Tahnee disconnected and looked into the incredible green eyes of the guy she hoped would rock her world tonight.

'Sorry about that. My friend Nina checking up on me. You're right on time,' she said, thrusting out her hip and smoothing a hand over her shimmering green top and tight denim skirt, a teasing move designed to entice, as she enjoyed the appreciative once-over he gave her.

'You look great,' he said, his sexy smile setting her pulse racing instantly.

'Glad you noticed, considering I've gone to way too much trouble with my make-up, though I guess the teenybopper ponytail sort of spoils the whole look, huh?'

She was babbling, her mouth running at a million miles an hour, anything to cover her nerves and the fact that a whole farm of butterflies was flapping madly in her belly.

'I like the ponytail. It's kinda cute.'

He reached out and tugged it, a gentle, barely-there tug that set her scalp tingling along with the rest of her. 'As for the make-up, I appreciate the effort you went to, but, seriously, you don't need it. You're gorgeous without it.'

'You sweet-talker, you,' she said, his gallant words more than making up for his grouchy behaviour of the first few days.

'So, where are we going?'

His smile had slipped and his shoulders stiffened; she wondered if he'd always been this anti-social or was it merely an after-effect of too much schmoozing in his finance days?

'Don't sound so enthusiastic,' she said, hoping he'd go for her idea and actually loosen up enough to enjoy it.

'You know I don't get out much. Guess I'm a bit concerned what your version of the casual dinner thing is?'

'Don't worry, my anti-social friend. We're going somewhere quiet—it shouldn't offend your sensibilities.'

She spoke in a fake posh voice and tilted her nose in the air, peeking at him from beneath long lashes.

He chuckled. 'In that case, how can I refuse?'

'I knew you couldn't,' she said, her expression smug as she grabbed her purse and hustled him out the door. 'It's part of my charm.'

'What? Guys not saying no to you?'

'There are no guys. Haven't been for a while, actually.'

Wasn't that the sad truth!

'Same here.'

For one, long moment, they connected. Here was a guy who knew about loneliness and, as much as he gave her the whole 'creative genius needs his privacy' spiel, she still didn't understand how a gorgeous, intelligent guy like Bo had managed to escape having a string of drooling women at his feet.

'So, no guys for you, either; well, I guess this get-up is wasted, then.'

She waved a hand at her outfit and this time, his stare lingered in all the right places, particularly her long, tanned legs, which she'd slathered in sparkly moisturiser.

'Are you always this smart-mouthed?'

'You like my mouth?'

She puckered up and for a moment she could see the gleam in his eye as if he was tempted to teach her a lesson, a very sexy lesson, she hoped.

'A lady never fishes for compliments.'

'And a gentleman wouldn't need prompting to pay them.'

She shut the door and flounced ahead of him, leaving him trailing after her like a servant after a queen.

CHAPTER NINE

Wally hadn't eaten under the stars for a long time. By this time of night, he'd usually burrowed in, having a nice hot cup of cocoa and reading his favourite book. Not tonight. Wally felt confused. He liked having Kaz around. He liked having a new friend. But she kept surprising him. Kaz had taken him on a picnic to his favourite watering hole and she'd been extra nice to him, but all he could think about was going home to bed. And he wasn't even tired!
Bo Bradford's blog, Wednesday evening.

'HOPE YOU like anchovies.'

Tahnee rummaged through the picnic basket, searching for the little glass jar housing one of her favourite acquired tastes.

Though her question sounded innocuous enough, she waited with bated breath for Bo's answer. She'd asked a few guys the same question and it had become a screening tool used to weed out the good from the bad.

The good guys always responded in the affirmative and they had more than a few dates. The duds hated anchovies and proceeded to either tell her why or treat her like a weirdo for liking them.

'Are you kidding? I love them.'

She sighed, muttered 'thank you, Lord' and finally found the jar, holding it aloft like an Olympic gold-medal winner.

'Good. I didn't know if you would or not so I brought a jar rather than slathering them on the pizza rolls.'

'Smart girl,' he said, his simple praise making her glow.

Could she get any more pathetic?

'So, you don't mind the picnic thing?'

Yeah, she could. Getting his approval was one thing, asking for it another.

He smiled the kind of warm, genuine smile that lit her from within. 'Mind? This is great. I can't remember the last time I've been here, let alone had a picnic.'

'This is one of my favourite spots when I come down to Sydney.'

She stared at the lights twinkling on Sydney Harbour, enjoying the hustle and bustle of a warm summer evening. The Manly ferry jostled for space alongside pleasure cruisers, water taxis carrying passengers and the dinner cruises that were packed with happy people toasting each other on deck. Though she loved Stockton, Sydney had a vibe she adored and for her it centred on the water.

'I thought you were a country girl, born and bred?'

'Stockton's not country! Though I guess a city slicker like you would think that.'

As for the born and bred part, he had no idea.

Determined not to go down the miserable road of her earlier childhood, she said, 'You've always been a Sydney boy?'

'Yes.'

No elaboration, no explanation. Guess she wasn't the only one who didn't want to talk about the past.

'Here, have another mini-quiche.'

She thrust the container holding the most exquisite sun-dried-tomato and fetta quiches she'd ever tasted under his nose, hoping the food would distract him from the awkward silence descending over them.

'Real men don't eat quiche,' he said, taking two anyway.

'Trust me, you're real enough.'

Tahnee stopped dead, hand midway between mouth and container. Surely her thought hadn't popped out into actual words?

'I'll take that as a compliment,' he said, raising his mini-quiche in a toast towards her and she blushed, thankful for the descending dusk and quickly stuffing a quiche into her mouth before she said anything else incriminating.

They ate in companionable silence for a while and she wondered when she'd last felt this relaxed in a guy's company. Usually, first dates entailed being at a restaurant, sitting across the table from some overconfident jerk with a high opinion of himself, being bored senseless by stories of his football prowess or the size of his portfolio.

When had she started viewing this as a first date?

Okay, maybe they hadn't spelled it out as such, but the way they'd been flirting earlier that day, his proposal of last night still lingering between them, he'd have to be thick as a brick wall not to cotton on to the fact she was coming around to his way of thinking.

Though what did he expect her to do? Fall into his arms without a prelude?

'You didn't have to go to all this trouble,' he said and she started, wondering if he'd read her mind.

'No trouble. Picking up the phone and ordering a gourmet picnic isn't exactly rocket science.'

Figuring out what to wear had been the hard part, requiring a degree.

'What I meant to say was I know we had that strange conversation this morning about rules and flings and stuff, but don't feel like I expect anything from you.'

He folded his forearms and rested them on his knees, leaning forward to pin her with a steady stare. 'I put you in an awkward spot by kissing you and then following up with that not-so-classy proposition, and I'm sorry.'

'Don't be,' she said, her heart sinking.

Once she'd got over her initial reticence—and finally admitted she liked him enough to ignore her previous reservations and take what she could for the short time they had together—she wasn't sorry, but it was pretty obvious he was and was trying to back-pedal faster than a runaway bride.

'It's not that I'm not attracted to you, because we both know that's a given considering what's happened so far, but I don't want to jeopardise our working relationship.'

His level-headed rationale made perfect sense and she'd considered the same drawbacks of getting involved with her boss. But she couldn't help it. She'd never been this drawn to anyone before and a huge part of her wanted to throw caution to the wind and jump him, right here, right now.

'I've only just found you,' he added, softening the blow with another sexy smile designed just for her.

Great. He wasn't making this easy on her.

When in doubt, she opted for bluntness. If the sensible one didn't like it, too bad.

'You're attracted to me, right?'

'I've just said so, haven't I?'

'Don't answer my question with a question.' She sounded exceedingly snippy and lightened up with a tremulous smile. 'You enjoyed the kiss at the Opera House?'

'It was amazing.'

Okay, so his admission came out in a grumpy, reluctant mutter but she couldn't blame him. He was trying to defuse their situation, she was trying to inflame it.

'And correct me if I'm wrong, but didn't you propose some pretty clear ground rules if we were to get involved, one of which was to not let anything affect our work?'

'I did.'

His eyes glowed emerald in the dusk and, in that moment, she knew she had him. Figuratively, at least; she was working darn hard on the literally part.

'Okay, then. Stop back-pedalling.'

She leaned back on her elbows, going for the knock-out move: chest out, hair toss, seductive smile, the body language equivalent of 'take me.'

'What's the problem, then? From where I'm sitting, things are looking pretty good.'

His gaze raked over her, lingering on her breasts, skimming her legs, focusing on her mouth. 'They look sensational from where I'm sitting.'

'In that case, what are we waiting for?'

She sat up and began packing up the remnants of their picnic dinner like a wind-up doll on double speed, eager to get back to the mansion before he changed his mind.

Bo laughed and helped her stack the plates and containers. 'What about dessert?'

'You're looking at it,' she murmured, caressing his cheek with the briefest of touches designed to entice.

'Good, I'm still starving,' he said, capturing her hand, raising it to his lips and planting a scorching kiss on her palm, sending the last of their doubts and second-guessing up in smoke.

Bo flicked on the light switch, dumped the picnic basket on the kitchen table and cast a desperate glance around the room in search of more camouflage.

The picnic basket had been good while it lasted, but now he couldn't hold it in front of him any more, he was exposed. Having the hard-on to end all hard-ons made him feel pretty good about himself, but it also made him feel like a randy teenager about to lose his virginity when Tahnee strolled into the kitchen, all five foot seven of perfection.

'So...here we are again.'

She propped herself against the table in a deliberate provocative pose, similar to how she'd conquered his lingering resistance at the Point. Her round breasts thrust forward, the hard nubs of her nipples prominent through the silky top, which shimmered from basic green to cerulean when she moved, her lips pouting, her shaded eyes glittering with seductive promise.

He was a goner.

'Would you like something to drink?'

She shook her head, tugged on the band holding her ponytail up and let her hair fall free in one, glossy golden curtain. He made some sort of sound—whether a gasp or a groan he wasn't sure—and her lips curved in a sexy little smile because of it.

'I thought you wanted dessert?'

She took a step forward and his gaze riveted to her leg, the way her hip and knee flexed in perfect synchronicity, how her thigh muscle tightened against the denim and how smooth the skin extending from her knee to ankle looked. He'd always been a leg man and Tahnee's didn't disappoint.

'I do,' he said, shifting behind a chair before she spotted exactly how much.

'Good. I'm partial to chocolate myself.'

He watched her sashay across the kitchen, flick on the kettle, fill a bowl with parboiled water and place a chocolate topping bottle in it.

'I didn't think I owned any chocolate topping.'

'You didn't. I asked the gourmet place to drop it around specifically when they brought the picnic.'

So she'd actually meant dessert rather than...well, *dessert*. Maybe it had been far too long since he'd done this because he had no idea what was going on and he was tying himself up in knots trying to figure it out.

'Ah, slight problem. I don't have any ice cream.'

She looked up then, her gaze hotter than molten lava, her smile slow and sexy.

'Who said anything about needing ice cream?'

Bo stared at her, blood pounding through his body as he wavered between shock and anticipation. Call him boring, but he'd always been a straight-up kind of guy when it came to sex. Sure, he liked mixing up the positions and he loved oral, but he'd never tried the whole eating food off each other thing.

Looked like he was about to expand on his education.

She laughed at his expression, which he tried to twist into something cool, but probably looked as dumbfounded as he felt. 'Don't worry. The chocolate is about as kinky as it gets.'

He didn't want to know about her past. In fact, the thought of her with other guys made him strangely angry when he had no right to be. But the minute she'd pulled out the topping bottle and said it wasn't for ice cream, a sense of inadequacy crept over him.

Yeah, yeah, it was a typical guy thing and he'd kick himself in the morning if he screwed this up tonight, but he had to know what she expected from him. The topping might be fun to try, but he'd draw the line at swinging from the chandeliers.

Well, at least till he knew her better.

'At the risk of sounding like a jerk, I'm not sure what you expect apart from the chocolate thing,' he finished lamely, hating the amusement in her eyes and feeling like a fool.

'Relax,' she said, picking up the bottle, testing it for temperature, and, apparently unsatisfied—which is what he would be very shortly if he mucked this up—submerged it again. 'Want to know a secret?'

'Uh...sure.'

Schmuck! Now she'd be telling him goodness knows what about her sexual past and he'd know he couldn't match up. Hell, his hard-on wilted just thinking about it.

'I've never done this before.'

'What?'

For a horrifying second, he thought she meant she was a virgin and there was no way he'd be responsible for deflowering her and possibly ruining the best working relationship he'd ever had.

She nibbled on her bottom lip, a nervous habit he'd noticed, and a small part of him was glad her uncertainty matched his own to a degree.

'The chocolate topping thing, I've never done it before. I read about it in this really hot mystery and ever since it's been something I wanted to try.'

'Oh.'

Suddenly, it hit him.

Why would she trust him, a guy she barely knew, to

indulge in this particular fantasy? Was it because of the ground rules they'd set down, about the non-permanence of their arrangement? Even so, they hadn't even had sex yet and she was getting into some pretty intimate stuff.

He should be flattered by her trust, but it left him more confused than ever.

'You're wondering why I'm doing this when we haven't…done it yet?'

'Yeah,' he said, grateful for her honesty.

He'd never met a woman so up front before and it was a refreshing change.

She looked him straight in the eye. 'Because I think we have a connection. Because I wouldn't even consider sleeping with you unless we didn't. Because I trust you. And, best of all, you have the perfect criteria for using chocolate topping and I saw most of it this morning when you got out of the pool.'

Her simple honesty made him feel ten feet tall and he crossed the space separating them, held out his arms and stifled a soppy sigh when she slid into them.

Less than two weeks, he had to remember that.

He didn't do connections, he didn't want the emotional links that bound two people together.

When she'd mentioned a connection, he knew she was talking about the physical attraction they'd already discussed.

That, he could do. As for anything else, he'd make sure he retreated behind his privacy once this was over.

If their working relationship worked out—and he

had a strong feeling it would—Tahnee would head back to her home town and they'd work by correspondence. His agent had already mentioned she usually worked that way and now he could see it was the perfect solution for both of them.

Have just under a fortnight of getting connected on a physical and professional level and maintaining a work relationship from afar after that.

Yeah, it could work, and thankfully she'd gone for his rule about nothing beyond the two weeks.

He had it made.

Then why the little voice that whispered he was getting in over his head?

'You think I'm a freak, don't you?' she murmured against his chest and he pulled back, placed a finger under her chin and tilted her face up.

'I think you're incredible.'

He feathered his thumb along her bottom lip, loving the way her pupils dilated and her lips parted on a soft sigh.

'I've never met anyone like you before.'

Her lips curved upwards, slowly, tentatively. 'That's a good thing?'

'You bet,' he said, using every ounce of self-control to lower his head slowly and graze her lips with his when, in fact, he wanted to devour her.

'You kiss real good for a hermit,' she murmured, trailing her lips along his jaw before returning to his mouth.

'You'd be surprised what other stuff us hermits are good at.'

He backed her up against the bench, sliding his hands into her hair, savouring the silky texture while pressing into her, his hard erection against her soft pelvis.

'This is it. Last chance to back out, change the ground rules, come to your senses, whatever,' he said, lifting her hair off the nape of her neck and nibbling his way downwards towards her collarbone.

'I'll take the whatever.'

His head lifted, their gazes locked and time stood still with the heady anticipation of what they were about to do.

'Come with me.'

He grabbed her hand and made for the door, unable to stand one more minute of torture. His new personal definition of torture: the two of them standing here deliberating with clothes on when he wanted her naked and moaning in his arms, and him buried deep within her.

'We forgot the chocolate,' she said, keeping in perfect step with him and not pausing for a second.

'Later.'

They had all night. They had the rest of the week and the next and he intended to make every minute count with the woman who'd made him lose his mind.

She laughed in wild abandon as they made a run for his room, their feet barely touching the polished floor boards.

'Lucky that toe's all better,' he said, fumbling with the door knob for a second before flinging open his bedroom door, and they tumbled into the room together.

'Yeah, must've been your magic touch.'

She stopped and tugged him to her for a swift, passionate kiss, igniting the raging inferno of need simmering between them in a second.

'You ain't seen nothing yet,' he murmured, working his way down the elegant column of her neck to her tantalising cleavage, which had teased him all night.

'Oh…'

She arched into him, offering her breasts and her body and he wondered how on earth he'd got so lucky.

'I could do this all night long.'

He licked his way across the swell of her breasts spilling out of her bra, unzipping the silky top with fingers turned into thumbs, wanting to prolong the unveiling of her beauty like a Master with an exquisite painting, but knowing he didn't have that much patience.

He wanted to see her, all of her, to feast his eyes, to slake his thirst for her.

The scrap of top pooled at her feet and his lips slowed momentarily as he traced the outline of her hard nipples through the sheer black lace bra with his fingertip.

'You are so sexy,' he said, replacing his fingertip with his mouth, suckling her, laving her, fired by her moans and his need.

'More,' she gasped as he lifted his head and blew on her dampened skin, watching her nipples pebble into tighter, firmer buds.

He smiled, knowing he'd never seen anything so tempting as the blond goddess before him, her hair tumbling in disarray around her shoulders, her breasts clearly visible through the barely-there bra and her lips parted and swollen and asking for more.

'Stop grinning like a Cheshire cat and make love to me,' she ordered, squaring her shoulders, which only served to thrust her breasts farther in his face.

'Bossy, bossy, bossy.'

Before she could react, he swept her into his arms and deposited her on the bed, enjoying her surprised 'oomph' as she stared up at him, tousled and blushing and absolutely ravishing.

'That's some move,' she said, reaching up to trace his lips with her fingers, staring at him in wonderment as if she couldn't quite believe this was happening.

'I'll show you moves.'

As Bo slid on top of her, Tahnee closed her eyes, giving herself up to the pleasure of exploring by touch.

She ran her fingertips over the faint stubble darkening his jaw, over the soft cotton of his polo shirt and lower to the expanse of firm skin where his shirt had ridden up.

Lower still, to the waistband of his jeans where her fingers inveigled their way in, but couldn't move farther due to their position.

'You're wearing too many clothes,' she grumbled, tugging impatiently at his button and zip, skimming her hand over the impressive bulge beneath.

'So are you.'

He rolled off her and she opened her eyes, not wanting to miss this show. Though she'd seen most of Bo's body that morning, it would be nothing on a first-hand private showing up close and personal.

'You first.'

'Okay.'

He whipped his polo shirt over his head in record time and she sighed, running her hands over the firm planes of his chest and abdomen. He had a serious six-pack going on, the type of abs seen on elite athletes rather than authors, and she vowed never to judge a book by its cover ever again.

'Want some help?'

She tugged at his zipper, inching it down tooth by tooth with an unsteady hand before slipping in to cup him, empowered by her boldness while heat scorched her cheeks.

It looked like her inner floozie had come out to play in a big way!

'Oh, my god,' he said, closing his eyes with a tortured expression on his face. 'If you want to see some of those moves I promised you, enough of that for now.'

'What? No staying power?'

She stroked his length once, twice, and chuckled as he growled and forcibly removed her hand from his open fly.

'I'll show you staying power.'

He had whipped off her skirt before she could blink and as he shimmied his way down her body, the determined glint in his eye setting her pulse hammering in her veins.

For her, the build-up was everything and it looked like Bo was into foreplay as much as she was.

However, when his mouth settled over her mound and he breathed on her, hot and heavy, she knew this would be no ordinary foreplay.

Unlike the few times she'd had sex in the past, he was

taking his time, not ripping off her underwear with the sole aim of satisfying his own desire.

Uh-uh, Bo had other ideas as he plucked at the elastic of her lace panties, his fingers skimming the skin underneath while his mouth continued to press against her most intimate spot.

Spirals warred with stars, dancing before her eyes, her vision blurring when he finally tugged her panties down and flicked her aroused clitoris with his tongue in one glorious sweep.

'Oh, yeah,' she moaned, her legs falling apart as he buried his head between them, licking her, stroking her wet folds and sucking her till she almost passed out with the intensity of it.

As the ripples built and her body stiffened, he didn't let up, increasing the pace, flicking his tongue in circles, sucking her till she bucked off the bed and screamed his name.

'Wow,' she muttered an eternity later, when the aftershocks had subsided and she lay limp against the damp sheets, stunned, stupefied and deliciously satisfied.

'You're beautiful,' he said, joining her at the head of the bed again, stroking her hair back from her face and staring at her with such awe that tears burned the back of her eyes.

'And you're very talented.'

She pulled his head down for a kiss, terrified she'd do something silly like cry if he continued to stare at her like that.

She kissed him with a hunger born of looking and

not touching for too many days and she barely managed to stop devouring him by gently disengaging her lips and pointing to his legs.

'One of us is still overdressed.'

He grinned and had his jeans and briefs off in one, smooth movement.

'Not any more.'

Her heart hammered like a piston as she stared at his body, every glorious exposed inch of it; and several very impressive inches in between.

He grinned at her blatant ogling, propped on an elbow in a classic centrefold pose.

'See anything you like?'

'Don't fish for compliments. It's not very manly.'

She forced herself to look away and to try to act casual as if the sight of his tanned, hard body didn't do it for her. As if.

'I'll show you manly.'

Slipping his arms around her, he rolled onto his back and pulled her with him till their bodies lay plastered skin to hot bare skin.

'I like being on top,' she said, nuzzling his neck till he purred.

'I like you being there.'

He shifted his hips in a little mock thrust, showing her exactly how much.

'So what about showing me some of those famous moves you were talking about earlier?' she said as she wriggled on top of him, delighting in the blissful expression sweeping his face.

'What did you think of the first one?'

'By the decibel of how I shouted your name, I think you know.'

Hopefully, the rest of Rose Bay hadn't also heard her approval.

Slanting his lips across hers, he probed her mouth with his tongue, daring her to meet him, to join him in another bone-melting kiss, and she gave as good as she got, her bones liquefying with not much coercion at all.

'You wanted moves? How's this?'

He yanked a bedside drawer opened, ripped open a foil packet and lifted her hips gently, sheathing himself while they both looked on.

She was vigilant with protection, but once again the guys she'd been with had made short work of it, fumbling and grumbling while Bo made an art form of it.

'Not bad,' she said, 'but I've got a few moves of my own I'd like to show you.'

'Be my guest.'

His hands hovered on her hips, his eyes blazed a trail down her body, lingering where their bodies almost joined. Almost, but not quite, and she desperately wanted to change that.

With infinite slowness, she settled over his shaft and lowered herself, one exquisite inch at a time, watching his face contort with passion and desire, more empowered than she'd ever been in her life.

She did this to him.

She turned him on, she gave him pleasure and once

she'd expanded to take him in fully and settled on top of him, she didn't want this feeling to ever end.

'You're so tight,' he breathed, his hands wandering up her body to cup her breasts, his thumbs skimming her peaked nipples, sending ripples of excitement through her.

'Want to help me loosen up?'

He matched her smile and they stayed like that, grinning like a couple of goofballs as she started to slide up and down, taking the lead, setting the pace and revelling in the build-up all over again.

Tahnee didn't know how long he thrust for, how long she rode him, but their pace quickened to match their breathing, a fine sheen of sweat slicked their skins and as her muscles contracted around him, she gave herself over to the astounding pleasure of making love with the first guy to blow her mind.

'Tahnee, Tahnee…'

Her name tumbled from his lips in frantic groans as he spilled into her and as she collapsed on his chest and he cradled her tightly, she suddenly wondered how she could walk away from something this good.

CHAPTER TEN

Wally had walked around the muddy water-hole three times, two more laps than his usual daily exercise. He had a lot of energy today and he was tired of staying at home and digging. He needed some air. He needed a break from Kaz, who had cast some type of weird spell over him. She talked and laughed and smiled way too much. Now he had a headache.
Bo Bradford's blog, Sunday.

'I CAN'T believe you drove up here just for a coffee.'

Tahnee tipped two sugars into her short black and stirred, more than a little grateful Nina had showed up. She needed someone to talk to, and chatting on the phone or sending SMS didn't cut it for what she had to say.

'Come on, T., you know me better than that. I can get a great caramel cappa back in Stockton. I'm here for the low-down. First-hand, unabridged, unadulterated, so spill.'

'How's—?'

'Uh-uh.' Nina held up her hand. 'You've asked about the kids, you've asked about Karl, you know Daisy is fine and Carissa's shop is doing better than ever while she's away. You can't possibly want to know about anyone else back home, so how about you cut to the chase and put your poor, gossip-deprived friend out of her misery?'

'I was only going to ask how the plans for Karl's surprise party are coming along. Sheesh.'

'Fine. Now, where were we?'

Tahnee chuckled at Nina's fierce mock frown.

'We were about to discuss my new job.'

Nina rolled her eyes. 'I bet the new job is fine, too. Besides, you're super-talented and even blind Freddy could see it. How's Bo?'

Ah…the million-dollar question.

The way she looked at it, Bo was mighty fine: smart, good looking, intelligent and an absolute tiger in bed. She'd never had it so good.

Then why the constant nagging doubt that something wasn't right?

'Bo's incredible.'

There, she'd admitted it to another person and the sky hadn't fallen in, lightning hadn't struck, though it looked like a bolt of Nina's over-enthusiastic advice could be just as bad.

'I knew it. Something's going on.'

'Or something's coming off, depending on your point of view,' she said, unable to keep the smirk off her face.

'You trollop.' Nina grinned from ear to ear. 'Details, please.'

Tahnee blushed just thinking about some of those 'details' and switched the conversation before she melted in a heap just from the memories.

'Honestly? He's fabulous. We work together all day and it's magic. He's creative and demanding, but I like that. I like working with the author one on one, it gives me a new perspective on my illustrations.'

By the sly glint in Nina's eyes, she knew what was coming before her friend opened her mouth.

'And after work?'

'That's pretty magical, too,' she admitted, wondering how she could put into words how special Bo made her feel and knowing she'd come up empty no matter how hard she tried.

'I've never met anyone like him before.'

'Wow, it sounds serious.' The cheeky gleam in Nina's eyes faded to be replaced by the usual concern.

'It's not.'

Far from it—they'd established that when she'd accepted the ground rules he'd laid out earlier in the week, which, of course, he'd been only too happy to go along with.

After all, what guy wouldn't? With her offering commitment-free sex as an added bonus to her stay, he probably thought all his Christmases and birthdays had come at once.

It should've been the perfect situation for both of them, though, somehow, the more time they spent together the more she wondered if she'd made a terrible mistake.

Not in sleeping with Bo; she'd never regret the magic

they created in bed. No, it had more to do with the two-week-only stipulation to their fling that had her banging her head against a wall.

Why should something this great end so soon?

Why shouldn't they try to make a go of it despite their differences?

It wasn't like she expected the family and white-picket fence tomorrow. She could have some serious fun with Bo, could explore and develop what they had; who knew, maybe an anti-social guy could change.

'You're in love with him.'

Nina said it softly, calmly, presenting the out-there statement very matter of factly. Tahnee took several gulps of scalding coffee before replying.

'You can't fall for someone in a week.'

'Really? I fell for Karl in about that time.'

Tahnee snorted. 'Puh-lease. You two took months to sort out your relationship.'

'And whose fault was that?'

Nina absentmindedly stirred her coffee, a goofy expression on her fact. 'I knew he was the one the minute I saw him sliding out from under my car. Not my fault he took longer to come to his senses.'

'That's not the point.'

Tahnee waved aside Nina's personal example of romance at its best. 'We're not talking about love here. I like the guy, that's all.'

'You sure there's not more to it?'

'Of course I'm not sure,' she snapped, immediately regretting her outburst and mouthing 'sorry' to her friend.

'Look at me, I'm a mess. I don't know what to wear in the mornings any more, I actually wear gloss every day and I find myself doodling. Me! The queen of anti-doodlers.'

The corners of Nina's mouth twitched and she quickly lifted her mug to conceal her smile. 'As long as it's not initials in hearts, doodling is perfectly normal.'

'No, it's not. It's crazy behaviour. It's the warped, twisted behaviour of someone in…like,' she finished lamely, unable to contemplate the horrific thought she could've fallen in love with Bo, let alone say it.

Nina reached across the table and squeezed her hand.

'Listen up. This is the best advice you're ever going to get on the love issue. You don't choose to fall in love, it just happens. Often, you don't pick the guy, he just comes along one day and suddenly he's there and you can't imagine not being with him. Love isn't about hearts and flowers and romantic dinners. It's about following your instinct and acknowledging that feeling deep down inside that your life wouldn't be the same without that guy in it. Is that what you feel for Bo?'

Tahnee closed her eyes, tried to picture her life without Bo and rubbed at her tummy, willing the coffee she'd drunk to stay down.

She hadn't…

Oh, hell, she had!

'You'll be fine, just trust your instincts.'

Nina squeezed her hand once more before releasing it and Tahnee opened her eyes, mustering the nastiest glare she could summon.

'Hey, don't shoot the messenger. I'm only trying to help.'

Tahnee slumped, shocked to find tears stinging her eyes. 'I know. It just wasn't supposed to happen like this.'

It wasn't supposed to happen at all.

No matter how perfect Bo appeared, he wasn't the right guy for her. He'd virtually said as much, yet she'd gone ahead and fallen for him anyway.

How stupid could she be?

'Just go with the flow, okay?'

'Right…' she said, managing a wan smile for her friend.

Go with the flow, huh? Knowing her luck, she'd end up flowing right down the gurgler.

'Is that yours?'

ABBA's 'SOS' pealed out from her handbag and Tahnee grabbed her mobile and answered it.

'Tahnee speaking.'

'Hey, it's Bo.'

And just like that, heat spread through her body like molten honey.

'Hi. What's up?'

'Are you free tonight?'

'Yeah, sure.'

Okay, she could've played it a little cooler, maybe drawn out her response, pretended to check her diary, something like that? But, no, she had to practically jump down the phone at him.

'Great. I have a surprise for you. Maybe we can go down to The Rocks, have that coffee we didn't get around to after the awards night? And I might have a surprise for you later. What do you think?'

She thought it sounded like the best offer she'd had in ages. Apart from the naughty one he'd already made, the same one that had her melting at the sound of his low voice.

'Sounds fabulous. Thanks for asking.'

'No problem. Just thought I'd let you know well in advance.'

She smiled. He really was a thoughtful guy.

'Why? The shock of this surprise isn't going to kill me, is it?'

He hesitated for the first time and she imagined him sitting behind his desk, that tiny crease between his brows as he pondered her question. She adored that little crease; it made him look so studious, so focused.

'I certainly hope not. I've gotten used to having you around.'

Her heart tripped at the implied meaning behind his words.

Was he simply making a statement or did he like being with her as much as she loved being with him?

'Great,' she said, wanting to lean forward and thump her head on the table repeatedly for such a lame response.

Why couldn't she have said 'I like being with you, too,' or something to that affect?

Then again, she was just the illustrator. He was supposed to be the one with the way with words.

His deep chuckles washed over her and she shivered

despite the warm sunshine filtering through an umbrella shade.

'Okay, I'll see you later, then?'

'You sure will.'

She didn't know what prompted her to drop her tone and almost purr into the phone, but she got the desired response.

'Hurry.'

One simple word filled with promise and need and heat.

She hung up, sat back and picked up a napkin to fan her face.

'I don't need to ask who that was,' Nina said, smirking while she drained her coffee and reached for her purse.

'He has a surprise for me.'

'I just bet he does if your neon-pink cheeks are anything to go by.'

Tahnee's hands flew to her cheeks and she covered them with cool palms.

'Promise you won't breathe a word of how pathetic I am to anybody?'

'Promise,' Nina chuckled. 'Now, I must run. Daisy can only mind Callum till three, but you have fun with your sexy author, okay?'

'Yeah, okay.'

Tahnee pulled a face, already wondering what the surprise could be, hoping it wasn't her marching orders.

'Relax, T. Everything's going to be fine, you'll see.'

Tahnee returned Nina's fierce hug, hoping her friend was right.

* * *

'How's the book coming along?'

Bo glared at Tahnee while she propped on the corner of his desk, swinging her leg in a purely provocative action designed to grab his attention from the PC screen.

'Right on track, if a certain sexy illustrator would stop trying to distract me and get back to her work.'

'I will if you give me a hint what the surprise is.'

Bo shook his head and made a zipping motion with his hand over his lips.

'Come on, just one, tiny clue.'

She picked up Wally and Kaz, contorting them into rude sexual positions and laughing when he grabbed them out of her hand and rearranged them in a platonic configuration.

'No. Quit bugging me.'

'You sound awfully tense. Is something on your mind?'

Her deliberately husky voice had him sitting bolt upright, his eyes darkening with lust.

'The only thing on my mind is words about these fellas,' he said, his mouth twitching with amusement as she inched her foot closer to him with the aim to play footsies, though with an appendage a tad higher. 'The book's running ahead of schedule and I'd like to keep it that way.'

He slapped her foot away just as she'd been about to reach paydirt.

'Hey, you're not sticking to the rules. No play during work hours, remember?'

She pretended to pout, loving the way his eyes gleamed as they focused on her mouth as she'd intended.

'But it's Sunday and you told me to hurry back over the phone. You're a tease, dangling this hush-hush surprise in front of me, then making me wait till tonight.'

'Ah...but anticipation is half the fun,' he said, his arm shooting out and capturing her leg, giving it a gentle tug till she tumbled into his lap. 'Don't you think?'

She wriggled in his lap, loving the flare of excitement in his eyes, revelling in her power as a woman as she felt the hard evidence of how much he wanted her nestled snugly against her butt.

'I think you enjoy keeping me on the edge.'

'Too right,' he said, trailing his forefinger down her cheek, across her lips and lower, brushing the top of her breasts with the barest of touches.

'But for now, we must work. Otherwise no play later, and I know how much you want me.'

'Ha! Shows how much you know.'

She bounded out of his lap and sent a pointed glance at his groin. 'It's the other way around. You want me. *Real* bad.'

They laughed in unison and Tahnee turned away and strutted across the room to her couch, knowing she had as much chance of getting any work done for the rest of the afternoon as she had of forgetting Bo once her two weeks were up.

Absolutely none.

'It's worth it, you'll see,' he said, his voice low and filled with promise as she glared at him, unable to sustain her mock anger when all she wanted to do was head back to his desk, plop into his lap and show him a few surprises of her own.

'It better be,' she said, picking up her sketchpad and raising it as a barrier between them, trying to block out his deep chuckles and the compelling, magnetic draw of his eyes, burning with fire and need.

A need which was entirely mutual.

CHAPTER ELEVEN

After sharing a quiet drink with Kaz down by the water-hole, Wally didn't feel so good. Sure, he liked Kaz but she asked too many questions and wanted to talk all the time. Sometimes, a wombat just wanted to be on his own. Why couldn't a kangaroo understand that? He had to tell her. But what if he hurt her feelings? Boy, making a new friend was tough.
Bradford's blog, Sunday night.

SIPPING at her coffee, Tahnee tried not to stare at Bo. No mean feat considering the guy looked like a fantasy dream date in his black polo and dark jeans. She'd been practically drooling over him all night, her gaze riveted to his face while they chatted, trying to stay focused on what he was saying while her mind repeatedly drifted to the magic he wielded with those lips.

The guy was bad for her concentration; in a trendy café filled with cute guys, he stood out a step above them all.

Then again, she was biased.

'You're inhaling that coffee.'

Her gaze snapped up to his, amusement highlighting the golden flecks in a sea of green.

She'd never seen anyone with green eyes before, not the genuine, startling colour of Bo's, and their unique colour had her staring more than usual.

Nice excuse.

Yeah, well, she'd buy it.

'It's good,' she said, sending him her best flirty look over the rim of the tall glass. 'Lucky you made it a double.'

'I'm not surprised you're up all night with the amount of caffeine you drink.'

She saw the second his words registered, a slow, sexy smile spreading across his face as he recalled exactly what kept them both up at night.

'I haven't heard you complaining,' she said, setting her glass on the table and folding her arms, knowing the simple action would press her breasts together and act as an instant cleavage enhancer. It was a slick move she'd seen on some rom-com movie late one night to capture a guy's attention; by the widening of Bo's eyes, it worked. Not to mention that it was cheaper than a Wonderbra.

'I'm not,' he said, tearing his gaze away from her cleavage to shake his head. 'I know what you're up to, trying to distract me and get me home so you can have your way with me.'

Chuckling, she said, 'You caught me. Is my cheap and tawdry ploy working?'

His voice dropped lower, its husky timbre sending a warm thrill of anticipation through her.

'Oh, yeah, it's working all right. I'm trying really hard not to be a chauvinistic pig with my gaze fixed on your chest, but you're making it damn difficult.'

Thrilled with their banter, she leaned forward and did a little shimmy.

'What? These old things? Nothing you haven't seen before.'

Okay, so she was pushing her luck. The guy wasn't a saint and she really wanted to know what this surprise was before they headed back to his place, but seeing his pupils dilate, his tongue flick out to moisten his lips, she grew high on the adrenalin kick of turning him on.

She could tease him all night, resurrecting memories of how many times he'd seen her bare breasts, not to mention her naked body. Of how many times he'd kissed and licked his way over every inch of her skin, coming back for seconds like a man starved.

But then she'd be doing herself a disservice seeing that every time she teased him and elicited a response, her own desire flowed through her body like liquid lava: hot, swift and all-consuming.

'You're a bad girl.'

By the appreciative expression on his face, he loved it.

'You bring out that side of me.'

Suddenly, she realised how true her words were. None of the other guys she'd ever dated had made her feel so wanton, so uninhibited, like she could say anything and do anything. Then again, none of those guys had turned her on like Bo did.

And you hadn't fallen for any of those guys, either.
Good point.

'What's with the serious face?'

He reached across the table and captured her hand, his touch never failing to make her feel cherished, secure, two feelings she'd craved her whole life.

Her foster parents had gone a long way to alleviating her insecurities, but they never quite left her, the early childhood years of being forcibly separated from her sisters a lasting nightmarish imprint on her soul.

Stan had been a lot like Bo, actually, a quiet man who valued his privacy, who wasn't overly talkative at the best of times. In a way, he hadn't helped her feeling that she could lose her new parents and get kicked out on the street at any time. She'd loved Stan, but maybe if he'd been more demonstrative, more verbose with his emotions, she mightn't still be hung up over stability and needing to belong.

'Old memories,' she said, annoyed she could think so badly of Stan. Along with Doris, her foster parents had done their best in raising her. They'd loved her, even if they hadn't been overly demonstrative.

His hand slackened its grip. 'You're thinking about another guy?'

Rolling her eyes at his injured tone, she said, 'Your ego is safe for now. I was actually thinking about how nice this is, being here with you, holding hands. Makes me feel good.'

His rueful smile reached his eyes. 'But what's that got to do with old memories?'

Tahnee paused, wondering how much she should tell him. She'd been upfront with him till now, not wasting time beating around the bush when they had so little time together.

But what now? Was it too soon to talk about the possibility of an ongoing relationship beyond the two weeks? Was it time to change the rules?

Not wanting to spoil this evening—or the much-anticipated surprise—she decided to hold off on opening up completely. After all, they had time.

The rest of their lives, if she had any say in it.

She settled for telling him a partial truth.

'Feeling good in the moment brings up other good memories. You know the type of thing. Getting your first bike, baking cookies with your mum, waking up on Christmas morning. That's all I was thinking about, family stuff.'

If she'd thrown a bucket of iced water over Bo, it would've had a similar reaction. His face froze, his eyes dimmed and he slipped his hand away on the pretext of grabbing his coffee. Lame, considering he had nothing but dregs left in his cup.

'Actually, I don't know,' he said, gripping the cup like a lifebuoy. 'I guess you got to play happy families growing up, I didn't.'

'Want to talk about it?'

'Not much to tell.'

His harsh laugh saddened her as much as his expressionless face.

Maybe if he opened up about his family, she'd have

more chance of understanding him and, in turn, of getting closer to him.

After all, if they were to take their relationship to the next level, surely they needed to trust each other enough to talk about their pasts. She'd expect nothing less from her partner and as she watched Bo, frozen in his pensive silence, the first sliver of fear sent a shiver down her spine.

What if Bo was emotionally shut off, the type of guy who couldn't or wouldn't articulate his feelings? A guy like Stan? She couldn't live her life with that type of uncertainty any more. If she'd learned one thing growing up, it was to look out for herself, to not rely on other people.

However, it was easier said than done, and right now she needed Bo to wrap his arms around her and tell her everything would be okay. Instead, he sat there, immobile, moody, closed off, and her heart gave a frightened shudder.

'My folks were society people, hell-bent on schmoozing as much as possible. They loved Brennan and me, but we didn't get to see them much. Guess I hold a grudge for that. Then, when Mum died, I thought "what a waste".'

'But you hang out with your dad and Brennan sometimes, right?'

He nodded, some of the tension leaving him.

'Yeah. We're good buddies, even if I'm not in their boys' club anymore. My dad's cool, for an uptight banker, and Brennan is a party boy who never grew up.'

'You could've been like them,' she said, resisting the

urge to slap a hand across her mouth when she realised she'd spoken her thought out loud.

He smiled, fixing her with an appreciative stare.

'Yeah, but I'm not, thank goodness. You really speak your mind, don't you?'

She nodded, glad he found it an endearing quality rather than a pain as most guys usually did.

'What's the point of beating around the bush? Better to face things head-on.'

Like telling Bo how she felt.

Like telling him how much she wanted to give them a go beyond next week.

Like telling him he was the best thing that had ever happened to her.

Thankfully, he suddenly leaped out of his chair, grabbed her arm and tugged her towards the door.

'Hey, if this is your idea of providing an evening's entertainment, I'd like to see what you do for an encore.'

'I'll show you when we get back to my place,' he said, holding open the door for her, his smouldering stare leaving her in little doubt he would follow up on his bold promise.

'What about my surprise?'

'Soon,' he said, his lips brushing against hers for an exquisite, prolonged moment before he pulled away. 'Very soon.'

Bo remained silent on the drive home, deep in thought, pondering the drug-like trance Tahnee had him in most of the time. He was drawn to her like kids to his books;

a phenomenon he couldn't explain, but was grateful for just the same.

'You're in a hurry?'

Glancing down at the speedometer, he took his foot off the accelerator and slowed as the traffic light ahead turned red.

'Sorry. Mind on other things.'

'I bet,' she said in a sultry voice reminiscent of his favourite jazz singer. 'Looking forward to getting home, huh?'

Suddenly, warning bells clanged in his head. For some inexplicable reason, her slip of the tongue in saying 'home,' implying hers, too, made him wonder if there was more to their relationship than met the eye. He'd been quite clear on the ground rules and she'd been more than happy to stick to them.

No commitment. No hanging on beyond two weeks.

The perfect situation for both of them.

But something in the way the word 'home' rolled off her tongue, something in her happy glow, cued him in to the fact that maybe, just maybe, the rules had changed. And that scared the hell out of him.

'Am I ever.'

He played it cool, not wanting to jump to any conclusions, but once his anti-commitment antennae had gone up, he was having a difficult time switching off his mental alarm.

'Great, me, too.'

She paused, studying his face with an intensity that made him squirm. 'Is something wrong?'

Plenty, if he listened to his gut instinct, the same gut instinct that had woken him up to the foibles of the financial world. His instinct had served him well in the past and he'd be damned if he ignored it now; right at this minute, it was telling him that Tahnee wanted more from him than he could give.

Forcing a smile, he said, 'No, I'm fine. Probably just a bit shell-shocked from being surrounded by so many people at that café. You know I don't get out often.'

Thank goodness. Visiting trendy spots like the café he'd chosen tonight just because he thought she'd like it reminded him too much of his financier days when winning over the customer and coming out on top were the primary objectives, people or job satisfaction be damned.

Little wonder he'd traded his portfolio for a PC and a healthy dose of personal satisfaction.

Her puzzled frown didn't detract from her beauty one iota. On any other woman, a frown would've added unattractive wrinkles to her forehead. On Tahnee, a few lines made her all the cuter.

'You really are a recluse, aren't you?'

'Yeah, and proud of it.'

Dealing with a bunch of fictional animal characters was a hell of a lot better than dealing with a bunch of money-oriented phoneys on a daily basis.

Her frown didn't disappear. If anything, it intensified after his answer.

'I'm surprised a guy your age isn't out partying and whooping it up.'

'A guy my age?'

She rolled her eyes. 'Don't go fishing for compliments. What are you, mid-thirties max?'

'Thirty-four.'

She snapped her fingers. 'There you go. Why aren't you out there using your fame to pick up women and impress the heck out of everyone else? I don't get it.'

Bo didn't like questions, especially the probing questions that Tahnee was firing at him with both barrels.

This was why he lived like a recluse. Why delve into his motivation when he knew the reasons behind his withdrawing from society weren't all that exciting? He'd had a gutful of the rat-race, he'd wanted to set his own pace. Not particularly riveting.

Though he hazarded a guess she'd find his secret identity interesting—not that she'd ever find out.

Nobody would, just the way he'd intended when he hid away in his mansion five years ago.

He shrugged, deliberately voiding his voice of emotion, not wanting to give her a sniff of how he hated this type of interrogation.

'Nothing to get. I value my privacy. Authors are renowned for liking their own company, which is how they manage to keep their butts planted in chairs long enough to churn out books and meet deadlines. No big secret.'

She knew he was fobbing her off. He could see it in the quirk of her eyebrow, in the slight 'I'm not impressed' compression of her lips and the steady, unwavering stare.

Damn, what had happened to flirting a little over coffee, offering her a great job—his surprise which they hadn't got round to yet—and heading back to his place for more mind-blowing sex?

'I guess not,' she finally said, slipping her hand into his. 'Seeing as I'm willing to let you off the hook, how about you get this car moving? Particularly since the light has been green for the last minute.'

Muttering an exasperated, 'Thanks for the heads-up,' he turned left at the next intersection and headed for home.

'Race you to the bedroom?'

Her soft question rose over the filtered jazz filling the car and he speeded up.

'You're on,' he said, hoping, by the time she discovered her surprise, they weren't off.

Bo drove like a maniac, covering the distance between The Rocks and Rose Bay in record time. He drove like he had a demon on his tail, like a man possessed, but Tahnee didn't mind. In fact, it added to the thrill, the rush of being with a guy who did it for her in every way.

Stopping the car with a spray of gravel in front of the mansion, he ran around the car, opened her door and helped her out.

'You're in an awful hurry to get inside,' she said, raising up on tip-toes to mould her lips to his, unable to wait a second longer for that first, magical rush when they touched, when they kissed.

'I want you so badly,' he said, pulling her into his arms, burying his face in her hair. She sighed, inhaling the heady combination of spice and oak, the scent that lingered on his pillows, the scent that would linger in her memory long after she'd left.

If she left.

'Hmm...I can feel how much.'

She wriggled her hips, inflaming his desire, making his erection twitch with a reflex eagerness.

Straightening, he captured her chin in his hand and tilted her face up, staring into her eyes and she wondered if he could read the need in hers.

He didn't blink, he didn't speak, his fingers lightly caressing her cheek while his intense stare bored into her, almost compelling her to understand something she had no idea about.

'You okay?'

'Come inside and I'll show you how much,' he said, dropping a soft, lingering kiss on her lips before leading her up the front steps and into the house.

'You've been awfully quiet,' she said, slipping off her stilettos as the door shut, her sudden loss of height making her feel petite and in need of a great caveman to carry her upstairs and have his way with her.

'I'd rather be doing this than talking.'

Her breath left her lungs in a little whoosh as he plastered his mouth to hers, coaxing her response with the barest flick of his tongue. Her lips parted beneath his and he deepened the kiss, ravaging her mouth with pent-up desire and a wealth of skill she'd come to expect from their sensational love-making.

'Wow,' she murmured, her head falling back to expose her neck to him, and he kissed his way down to her breasts, nipping at her cleavage, sending shards of delight through her body.

Recapturing her mouth, he crushed his lips to hers in a hot, open-mouthed, smouldering kiss that left her weak and clinging to him.

Somehow, she sensed this wasn't a night for long, slow seductions. They'd been dancing around each other all day with subtle glances while working, playing word games designed to entice and prolong the desire that grew between them with every passing second.

She needed him too badly, right here, right now, his hands all over her, skimming the bare flesh on her back, cupping her butt, squeezing her against him.

'We're not going to make it to the bedroom, are we?'

Before he could respond, her hands slipped to his fly and she had him unzipped and out in a second.

'No,' he growled, backing her towards the nearest wall, ending their brief conversation with a blistering kiss, the type of kiss that preluded lose-your-mind-blow-the-consequences type of sex as he fumbled in his wallet and sheathed himself in the time it took for her to untie the knot holding her halter top up.

'Oh, yeah, Bo,' she gasped as he caressed her breasts, kneading them, cupping their fullness while flicking his thumb against her nipples.

Her heartbeat throbbed in her ears as she arched against him, his hands dropping to her skirt, bunching the cotton folds and yanking upwards till his erection nudged her panties.

He rubbed himself against her, once, twice, her low moan all the incentive he needed to rip the scrap of lace off her and nudge towards her slick entrance.

'This is going to be hard and fast,' he murmured, tearing his polo over his head, pressing against her, hot hard chest plastered to her searing skin as waves of unparalleled sensation rippled through her body.

She desperately needed more of him, her hunger fuelled by a mind-numbing lust she'd never anticipated in her wildest dreams and an overwhelming urgency to lose herself in the moment.

She'd never had sex like this before, the type of sex romance novels depicted, but were pure fiction as far as she was concerned, and, with a sexy, talented partner like Bo, she knew this encounter would far surpass any words generated on paper.

'Hard and fast is good,' she said, hooking her leg around his waist and pushing against him, her wet folds surrounding the tip of his penis before he knew what was happening.

'Tahnee,' he breathed, burying himself in her to the hilt, filling her as she gasped in ecstasy, transporting her to another plane as he withdrew and repeated the action, pumping into her with a speed designed for pleasure and pain and the ultimate satisfaction.

Her breathy moans fired him and he grabbed her butt, hoisted her up and held her against the wall as she wrapped her legs around him, effectively imprisoning him deep within her.

In and out, faster…faster…the friction building to a climax that threatened to shoot her into orbit and explode into a million stars.

She'd never felt like this, never felt so totally connected

to a guy before. As her hips ground against his, her mouth open and eager beneath his and she groaned her climax in a deep, guttural sound totally alien to her, she knew she would never forget this man, this time they'd shared.

Savouring their emotional connection almost as much as the physical, she squeezed him tighter as he surged towards climax, the pressure rebuilding in heart-stopping waves as he pounded into her, obliterating everything but this moment, this man and the ecstasy they created as he came along with her.

'Oh, my,' she said, leaning her head back against the wall, a sheen of sweat covering her face and her exposed breasts, her nipples thrusting towards him in hard pink peaks.

She should've been self-conscious but she wasn't. After all, what was there to hide from the man who had connected with her on so many levels, who'd taken her to heaven and back and who could keep her there if only he felt as much for her as she did for him?

'You okay?'

'Never better.'

She smiled, the smile of a satisfied woman and he grinned in return, making her feel like she'd just given him the best gift and he hadn't been disappointed when he'd ripped off the wrapping.

'Want to take a shower?'

He kissed her taut nipples and the sparks flared in an instant, the embers of their slaked passion needing little to re-combust.

'You're full of good ideas,' she said, burying her face

in his neck, savouring the closeness, staying wrapped around him as he carried her to the ensuite.

Wishing she could stay this close to him for ever.

Tahnee had died and gone to heaven.

Actually, she'd read somewhere that orgasms were like little deaths or some such thing. Well, in that case, she'd curled up her toes three times during the night...and how!

Rolling onto her side slowly so as not to wake Bo, she snuggled under the duvet, content to watch him sleep.

She'd never seen anything so beautiful as this incredible, handsome man lost in slumber, his long eyelashes casting spiky shadows on his cheeks, his beautiful mouth slightly tilted at the corners, his face, usually so animated, relaxed and peaceful.

Early morning sunlight filtered through the wooden blinds, bathing him in a diffuse, ethereal light, almost as if he wasn't real.

That would be just her luck, falling for a dream guy only to find he wasn't real.

Reaching out, she touched his naked chest and smiled. No, she wasn't hallucinating or delusional. Bo was all real and then some. She had the tender spots to prove it.

'Good morning.'

Her gaze drifted up from admiring the sculpted planes of his chest to meet his eyes, half-hooded and watching her with clear intent.

'Hey there, sleepyhead.'

She brushed her lips across his, not caring about morning breath or bed hair or anything else inconsequential. She was right where she wanted to be, waking up next to the sexiest guy in the world.

'Are you thinking what I'm thinking?'

'What's that?'

She snuggled closer, not requiring any mindreading skills to see where his mind was heading. She'd seen the glint in his eyes and could now feel the hard evidence prodding at her stomach.

'Oh, that! Not much thinking going on there, unless it's true what they say about guys, that their brains are located in their—'

'Hey, I've just woken up. Leave the insults till later, at least till we start work. You do realise it's Monday morning?'

Just like that, her mind lost track of making love and focused on the fact this was their last week together and she hadn't got around to broaching the subject of what happened at the end of it. In fact, her intentions to talk had gone by the wayside somewhere between a sensational short black coffee and barely making it through the front door before having the kind of sex that made a girl forget everything bar her name. And she was…?

'Don't remind me,' she said, rolling onto her back and flinging her forearm across her eyes. 'My boss is a slave driver and he won't understand if I'm late because I was caught up having nooky with this amazing guy.'

He tugged her forearm away, a huge grin on his face. 'You think I'm amazing?'

Oh, yeah…

Despite his anti-social quirks, Bo was one heck of a guy and she'd fallen for him in less time than it took her to decide what colour to paint her armoire.

Rolling her eyes in mock exasperation, she said, 'Don't let it go to your head.'

He glanced down at his erection, smug and proud. 'Too late for that.'

'You're such a male.'

She rolled onto her side and curled into him, squealing when he started tickling her, wishing this could go on for ever. Maybe it could if she ever got around to broaching the subject.

Calling 'truce,' she braced her hands on his chest to hold him off.

Yeah, like that would work if he wanted to overpower her and have his way with her, although that didn't sound so bad.

'Before we get too carried away, how about we get to that surprise I mentioned yesterday?'

She slapped her forehead. 'I can't believe I forgot in all the excitement.'

They grinned in unison, the glorious, joyous, satisfied smiles of two people who had got caught up in the 'excitement' several times last night.

'Is it in this room?'

She looked around while he covered her hands with his, plastering them against his hard chest, his heart thumping steadily beneath her palms as she wondered if he felt half as much for her as she did for him.

'You could say that,' he said, staring into her eyes

with the type of intent that had her conjuring up all sorts of wonderful dreams, particularly the best dream of all, the forever one.

'How about we extend our arrangement beyond the end of this week?'

Her heart stopped for a breathtaking moment before racing at a million beats a minute.

'Are you serious?'

She almost whispered the words, too afraid to speak louder in case she'd spoil the magical aura surrounding them. Bo had just uttered the words she'd hoped for and she couldn't believe it.

Laughing at her stunned expression, he said, 'Of course I'm serious. Surely you know you're the best illustrator in the business and I'd be a fool to let you go.'

Illustrator...best in the business...fool...

The words were like sharp pins stabbing at her bubble of happiness till she had nothing left but a deflated empty balloon of devastation.

One word stuck in her consciousness: fool.

Bo hadn't been the fool, she had, for forgetting his damn rules and losing her heart in the process.

'You're talking about extending my contract?'

'Of course. Just because you won't be here doesn't mean we can't work together. You already told me you worked from home for other authors—we can do the same. Great surprise, huh? So what do you say?'

I say you're crazy if you think I'm going to put myself through that.

Stupidly, she'd harboured the faintest hope that

maybe she'd got his initial offer wrong, that maybe he wanted her to stay around? However, he'd made it pretty clear: he was offering her a job, nothing else.

She would return to Stockton, he'd stay here and they would make one, big, happy book together. Several books, if they were lucky.

Well, she had news for him.

'I need some time to think about it.'

Time to get her emotions under control before she started blubbering like the deluded fool she was.

Time to get away from his potent presence and think about what refusing him could do to her career and ultimately her dream of owning her own home and a piece of lifetime security.

Most of all, time to mend her shattered heart.

His grip on her hands slackened off and she used the opportunity to slip her hands away on the pretext of twisting her messy hair into a top knot when in reality she couldn't bear to feel his heart pounding beneath her palms, the heart she would never have.

He frowned. 'You don't sound so thrilled.'

'It's not that—' She clamped her lips shut, wishing she'd had the sense to keep her mouth closed for once. In this case, her usual bluntness wouldn't be an asset, and, predictably, he pounced.

'Then what's up? I thought you'd want to continue our arrangement beyond the two weeks.'

Tahnee tried not to wince. It was the second time he'd called what they shared an 'arrangement' and she hated it.

What did she expect? He laid out the rules, she'd followed them. End of story.

But that was just it. She didn't want their story to end, not at the end of the week, not ever. She wanted the story to turn into a fairy tale with her and the greatest guy she'd ever met in the starring roles.

Yeah, like that was going to happen.

Suddenly, awareness flared in his eyes and his lips thinned into a hard line.

He knew.

Damn it, he'd twigged; she searched her brain for a quick way to throw him off the track, to pretend that she was fine with his offer, was fine with ending their relationship at the end of the week.

For that's exactly what it was: a relationship, not an arrangement. Bo could call it what he liked, could dress it up or dress it down, but they'd had more than a casual fling, no matter what he thought or how he callously described it.

'This isn't just about my job offer, is it?'

If his stricken expression was any indication, she'd hazard a guess he wasn't too thrilled at the idea.

Sighing, she said, 'No.'

'You agreed to the rules. What's changed?'

With razor-sharp precision, he zeroed in on what was bothering her. She should've been glad he was so tuned in to her feelings and had the guts to confront her rather than dance around the main issue like most guys would've.

However, how could she be glad when his eyes had hardened to a flinty green?

For one god-awful moment, her lower lip quivered. She couldn't cry. She wouldn't, but as the realisation sank in that he didn't want to have this conversation, let alone anything more to do with her, her eyes stung.

He didn't reach across to her.

He didn't caress her cheek with tenderness like he usually did or trace her lips like he'd never seen them before.

He didn't smile or wink or broach the distance between them that yawned across the bed as wide as the Simpson Desert.

He didn't do anything but stare at her with cool calculation, as if trying to gauge her mood, and she took a deep breath, hating herself for putting them in this position.

'Maybe I've changed,' she said, plucking at the sheet lying crumpled beneath them, a stark reminder of how many times it had twisted around or under them last night. 'Maybe always following rules isn't any fun.'

He didn't smile.

'Rules are made to protect people and in this case they were important. We didn't want to screw up our work, remember?'

A diffuse ache settled around her heart as she realised that work was his major concern. Not her or her feelings, but that she might not get his precious pictures finished if she turned into a woman scorned and flew into an hysterical tantrum. Jeez, didn't he give her any credit?

'This has nothing to do with work.'

Oops, her voice rose along with her blood pressure

and she softened it. They had to have this conversation, one way or another.

'This is about you and me and you know it.'

If his expression grew any bleaker, his face would freeze.

'I thought you were happy sticking to the rules. I didn't think you wanted more.'

'I've changed my mind.'

There, she'd said it, virtually admitting she was putty in his capable hands.

He shook his head, running a hand through his mussed hair. 'I can't give you what you want.'

His muttered words chilled her to the bone and she tugged the duvet higher, wishing she could snuggle into its warmth, pull it over her head and not come out till this whole disastrous fortnight was over.

He couldn't give her what she wanted?

Yeah, he'd got that right.

She wanted a guy to love her, to cherish her, to create a happy home with, to make babies with to fill that home with warmth and laughter and all the good things in life.

Most of all, she wanted rock-solid stability, something she'd never been certain of growing up. She wanted her guy to give her all that and more; by Bo's cold reaction, he wasn't that guy.

She could've let him off the hook completely, but a small part of her wanted to make him squirm.

'And what do you think I want?'

Pushing up to a sitting position, she clutched the duvet around her like a protective shield, hating how vulnerable she felt naked, though at least now she wasn't lying next to him all cosy and post-coital and morning-after.

The battle lines had been drawn and she needed every advantage she could get, even a small one like towering over his reclining figure.

'Don't do this, Tahnee.'

'Do what? Be honest about how I feel?'

She snapped her fingers, hoping her temper wouldn't follow suit. 'Oh, that's right. Honesty about feelings is a girl thing and I guess you wouldn't get that.'

'This is exactly what I didn't want to happen.'

He rolled away from her and out of bed, tugging on a pair of black boxers, but not before she'd had a mouth-watering eyeful of the best butt this side of the Pacific.

Not fair. He shouldn't be distracting her when they were about to have their first proper fight. Hmm... maybe they were heading into a relationship after all?

'I didn't expect this, either,' she said, relieved when he didn't walk out on her, wishing he'd pull a shirt over his head to keep her from staring at his broad chest, the same chest she'd licked and kissed and tickled so many times over the last week. 'And I'm not expecting anything from you. I just thought...when you said...' She trailed off, hating the distance between them, hating his defensive posture, which now included folded arms over his chest.

'I like you. I've had a great time this last week and we work really well together. By extending your contract, I thought you'd know how much I appreciate your talent, but as for anything else...' He shook his head, having the decency to look sad. 'I'm better off alone, let's just leave it at that.'

'Let's,' she snapped, bundling the duvet around her as she struggled to her feet, desperate to get out of the room before she bawled.

Head high, she stalked towards the door, trying to look as elegant as possible given the bulky burgundy-and-black-striped duvet wrapped around her.

'I'm sorry,' he said, his tone soft and dejected.

She didn't look back as she slammed the door on her way out.

CHAPTER TWELVE

Wally dug harder and harder. His claws scrabbled in the dirt, faster than ever before. Work was good. It kept his mind off other things, like the fight he'd had with Kaz. Wally didn't like it. Kaz had become his new best friend, so why did she have to make things so hard? He liked his own burrow. He didn't want her to move in. Why couldn't she understand a wombat needed space?
Bo Bradford's blog, Tuesday morning.

BO STARED at the blank computer screen, his fingers poised over the keyboard. He willed the words to come, cursed his silent muse and generally grew angrier as he realised he had his first full-blown case of writer's block.

It had never happened to him before. In fact, he didn't believe in it, a firm believer in the old adage that if you sat in the chair every day and made yourself write, you couldn't get blocked. Even if the work wasn't great, getting something down on the page was better than nothing. He could fix crap—he couldn't fix a blank page.

However, the longer he stared at the screen and the higher his blood pressure rose, he knew something had to give and right now he sure as hell couldn't afford it to be his productivity.

Pushing away from the desk, he grabbed his laptop case from underneath it. Maybe he needed a fresh environment, somewhere to stimulate his creativity away from the mundane routine of his office.

Maybe what he really needed was a...lobotomy.

Cursing his inner voice for its honesty, he shovelled writing pads and pens into his case, studiously avoiding looking at the couch opposite and the usual place he found his creative stimulus.

Not that Tahnee would've noticed if he jumped up on his desk and started doing the Mexican wave. She'd been just as careful to avoid glancing his way for the last half hour, her head bent over her sketchpad till he wondered if she'd fallen asleep.

Another four days of this: four whole days of awkward greetings, frigid silences and a sinking feeling that this entire fiasco was his fault.

Waking up next to her yesterday morning had been great. It had been the aftermath of their little conversation when he'd sprung his surprise on her that had shattered their friendship beyond repair. He'd decided to give her space and gone out for the day.

Okay, so 'give her space' could actually read he was too chicken to face any more deep and meaningful revelations, but it had done the trick. They hadn't seen each other all day and he'd half-expected her to have vanished by the time he got back. Yet here she was, reporting for duty the day after, looking incredibly sexy in a pair of tight denim jeans, a pink fitted T-shirt hugging the breasts he couldn't get enough of and her shiny blond hair loose around her shoulders, effectively screening her face from his curious glance.

And he was curious. He wanted to see her face, read her eyes, see what was going on in her head—in regard to their working relationship, of course.

Not that he was being intentionally callous, but he couldn't think beyond that, couldn't entertain the thought of having a full-blown relationship with someone who didn't know who he really was, let alone inflict his grouchy personality on another human being long term, especially someone as special as her.

'If you're going to stand there all day and watch me, I'd rather work somewhere else.'

She raised her head and looked straight at him, her blue eyes frosty.

Yep, he could get a reading now, clear as day, and the message read: rack off.

'I was just leaving,' he said, picking up his laptop case and hoisting the strap over his shoulder. 'Thought I'd work off-site today.'

She stared at him, the slight derisive curl of her lips telling him she knew he was running away.

'You only have two more scenes to write then we're done, right?'

He nodded, surprised by how much he hated the truth of what she'd said.

What if she didn't accept his offer? What if the way he'd bungled his way through her revelation of wanting more had driven an irreversible wedge between them?

'Two scenes, and that's it?'

Refocusing, he said, 'Yeah. You're so quick, we should be finished ahead of schedule.'

She bent her head again, her hair shielding her face. 'Good.'

That was it. One word uttered in a voice devoid of inflection or emotion, so he had no idea if she meant she was pleased about meeting the deadline or she couldn't wait to get the hell out of here.

And the worst part?

He didn't want to push her right now.

'I'll see you later,' he said, heading for the door, hating her grunted response, hating how it had come to this.

Tahnee stayed frozen till she heard the front door slam and Bo's car rev before unfolding her stiff legs from the sofa and padding across to the window, her bare feet enjoying the cold bite of the floorboards.

Her entire body ached from holding herself rigid for the last half hour, ever since he'd walked into the office and mumbled a greeting. She'd forced herself not to look up, not to move, to stay focused on her work. It was the only way she could stop herself from breaking down, snapping a pencil or throwing her entire box of charcoals at him.

Watching him race down the gravel drive and out of

the fancy wrought-iron front gate like he had the devil chasing him, she managed a sad smile.

Bo was running scared.

He'd avoided her the whole day yesterday and now it looked like more of the same. Shaking her head, she turned away from the window and plopped onto the couch, swinging her feet up and lying back with her head propped in her hands.

So what did she expect? He was a guy, wasn't he? The entire species had the running-away thing down pat. Must be in the genes.

Not that confronting him again would do any good. She'd tried to be honest and look where it had got her. On the verge of walking away from the best job opportunity ever, all because she'd been stupid enough to fall in love with the boss.

Cringing, she pummelled a cushion with her feet, hating how naïve it sounded, even if only in her own head.

She'd fallen in love with the boss.

How many times had she warned friends away from the perils of getting involved with workmates? Hence her agreeing to Bo's blunt ground rules, which clearly stated they wouldn't let it affect their working relationship.

But how many times had she seen the devastation first-hand when a work relationship soured?

Too many times in the brief stints she'd done as a waitress and retail assistant while studying for her art degree and she'd vowed to never go there.

Well, surprise, surprise, here she was, mired in her own little workplace drama, though this one was serious.

This one could cost her the dream she'd been striving for, the dream that meant everything.

She'd struggled for so long, saving every penny, but if the mud-brick cottage sold at next month's auction, which was more than likely, she wasn't sure if she could start again. It had taken her for ever to find the perfect house, the type of home she could fully make her own, the type of home that was the fulfillment of her dream for a lifetime of security.

And now she might have to throw it all away because she'd made one stupid mistake.

Love sucked. Big time.

Making a lightning-fast decision to drop everything and drive up to Stockton to take another look at her dream home, her own private comfort food, she leapt to her feet and flung the cushion at the couch.

However, her sporting prowess had always been on par with her cleaning skills, very average, and the cushion missed, hitting a pile of papers and magazines stacked on a small table behind it and sending them cascading to the floor.

Cursing this all-round crappy day, she kneeled down and started restacking the pile, wondering why Bo hadn't filed these along with the rest of his super-organised office. Then again, why should she care? It wasn't like she'd be working in here beyond the end of the week anyway.

Suddenly, her eyes settled on a cover pic of the *Financial Review* and she grabbed the magazine, a small picture catching her eye, making her want to take a closer look.

Wynn Burrell, the face of finance in Australia, the guy who owned half the country via his massive financial holdings, stared up at her.

The Burrells were huge, particularly in Sydney, and had been plastered on every magazine and newspaper from the *Wall Street Journal* to the *New York Times*, *Time* to *GQ*. Wynn's profile sold newspapers and magazines, not that she could blame the media. He had a striking face, not classically handsome, but more rugged with his large nose, chiselled cheekbones and penetrating green eyes.

Eyes the same colour as Bo's, featured in a tiny picture boxed to the right, the same tiny box that had captured her attention a minute ago. The same tiny box that proclaimed Bo as Wynn's son!

No way…

Quickly flipping to the accompanying article, she speed-read, her eyes scanning the print as fast as she could, eager to learn as much about the guy who obviously had more secrets than she had pairs of jeans.

The article centred on Wynn and his mega-success in the finance world, but towards the end there was speculation regarding Wynn 'The Whiz's' son Bogart, who was well on the way to following in dear dad's footsteps, but vanished from the business scene years ago without a word. Wynn said he was proud of his son and the choices he'd made and he expected the media to respect his privacy.

That was the gist of it and Tahnee flipped the magazine shut, her gaze drawn to Bo's picture.

Why hadn't he told her?

They'd chatted so many times about his past and his dad, yet he hadn't mentioned a word of his true identity.

'What's going on with you?' she muttered, rattling the magazine, wishing she could rattle some sense into Bo in the process.

Staring at his pic, she traced the outline of his confident, smiling face with her finger, wondering if she really knew this guy at all.

In actual fact, what did she know?

Bo didn't like socialising and had turned into a recluse.

Bo didn't like getting emotionally attached.

Bo was brilliant at his job, but lousy at relationships.

The weird thing was, now that she'd learned Wynn Burrell was Bo's father, several things clicked into place like toppling dominoes.

He valued his privacy? She could live with that.

He wanted to protect his identity? She could live with that, too.

He didn't trust her enough to tell her important stuff like who he really was? No way could she live with that.

Suddenly, a tiny flicker of hope ignited in her heart and burned brighter, fanned by a brilliant idea.

What if she could get Bo to open up to her, to realise she accepted him for who he was? Would that mean a possible future for them?

After yesterday morning, she never wanted to see the guy again, let alone admit her love for him, but now she couldn't ignore the possibility of obtaining her dream after all.

She'd already gone out on a limb.
What else did she have to lose?

Bo cursed when he swung into the drive and saw the kitchen light on.

Tahnee was up. When he'd come home at the same time last night, the house had been in darkness and he'd welcomed the silence as he'd slipped in unnoticed.

He didn't want to see her, especially in the kitchen, the place they'd sat around every night after work, drinking coffee, feigning interest in food before tearing each other's clothes off and barely making it to his room.

Parking the car, he switched off the ignition and grabbed his laptop. He couldn't ignore her for ever. They had three days left to work together, three days to make this book his best work ever, three days for him to work out what he'd do if she chose to walk out on him and leave him without an illustrator—and leave him with a gaping hole in his life, which he didn't want to think about just yet.

Eager to get the inevitable confrontation over and done with, he let himself into the house and stepped into the kitchen, every muscle in his body screaming 'run, get away while you still can,' because every time he saw Tahnee, he slipped further and further into a place he didn't want to go.

The place that painted this very picture before his eyes: a beautiful, warm, vibrant woman waiting for him in his cosy kitchen at the end of a long hard day.

A place which beckoned and could suck him in for ever if he let it.

'You're still up,' he said, stalking into the kitchen with all the finesse of an angry bear, dumping his laptop and heading for the fridge.

Not that he wanted anything to drink, but, if he didn't have something to fill his hands, he'd be tempted to grab hold of her and never let go.

She'd looked incredible earlier that morning, all fresh and sunny and vibrant, and it had taken all his will-power not to haul her into his arms, which was why he'd headed out to work for the day.

Work, ha! Like that would happen while his mind focused on one thing and one thing only: figuring out how to clean up the mess he'd made of his relationship with Tahnee.

'Hello to you, too,' she said, her voice a husky purr and his head snapped up, hitting the top shelf of the fridge.

What had happened to the frosty tone, the one he could deal with? She hadn't sounded like that since...well, since he'd been buried inside her, losing his mind.

Grabbing a soda, he swung to face her. 'What's with the tone?'

She widened her eyes ever so slightly, doing a great innocent act if he didn't already know better. For a girl who looked like butter wouldn't melt in her mouth, that same mouth was definitely built for sin.

'No tone. I just need to chat to you about some interesting publicity stuff I saw on you today.'

'Where?'

He ripped the tab off the soda and took several gulps, hoping to ease the tightness in his throat muscles, which had seized up the second he started focusing on her mouth.

'*The Financial Review.* The one with you and your dad on the cover.'

He choked on the fizzy bubbles, coughing and spluttering like a drowning man. Ironic, considering he felt like he was floundering way out of his depth the instant he'd heard she'd discovered his real identity.

Clearing his throat several times, he said, 'Guess we can add snooping to your résumé.'

Her silky smile didn't assuage his fear that there was more to this conversation about her discovery.

'If you don't want me to know who you really are, you shouldn't leave stuff lying around.'

She paused, her gaze suddenly steely. 'You should tell me.'

'It's not important,' he said, finishing off the soda and lobbing it into the trash, wishing he could slam dunk this conversation as easily.

'Not to you, obviously.'

She wasn't cutting him any slack, pinning him with a direct stare that could freeze ice in Antarctica.

Propping against a bench, he said, 'I've already told you I'm a private person. I barely know you—why would I divulge my true identity to you?'

She flinched as if he'd struck her and he gripped the bench before he wavered, lost resolve and rushed over there to comfort her, which was his first impulse.

He knew where this was leading now.

She wanted to push him to open up, to get him to acknowledge the feelings he had for her simmering away like a bubbling volcano ready to explode.

But he wouldn't let that happen.

He wouldn't do that to her.

She was too special for that, too special to be lumbered with a guy who couldn't give her half of what she wanted.

To her credit, she didn't bail him up about not knowing her, about belittling the incredible time they'd shared together. Instead, she blinked several times before resuming her killer look.

'Nice try, but I'm not going to let a little of your signature moodiness stop me. So you're a Burrell? Big deal. I don't see why it's a big secret.'

Damn it, he hated feeling like this, hated having to justify his motivations.

This is why he didn't do relationships.

This is why he'd really left the financier life behind.

He liked being on his own, he liked doing things his way.

Though he'd loved working alongside his old man and Brennan, he'd hated having to justify every little thing he did: to his boss, to the board, and to his dad, who had never questioned his judgement before.

Even as a kid, he'd been a loner, preferring to concoct stories in his head rather than play footy and though he was grateful for the hard years he'd put into finance, the years that had allowed him to get set up with this house to follow his dream to write in the first place, he didn't miss the whole 'why are you doing that, Bo?' routine.

Yet here he was, five years later, having to explain himself and it didn't sit well.

'No big secret. None of this is any of your business, that's why I didn't tell you.'

He pushed away from the bench and headed for the door. He didn't want to go through this any more, didn't want to say something he'd regret.

'Funny, I didn't pick you for a guy who'd run scared.'

He stopped dead and turned to face her. 'You don't know the first thing about me.'

To his surprise, she shot to her feet and crossed the short distance between them in a second, almost treading on his toes while she got in his face.

'That's bull. I know what I see and what I see is a guy who won't acknowledge any emotion whatsoever. A guy so wrapped up in hiding away from the world that he can't see what's standing right in front of him.'

'You want to know what I see standing in front of me? I'll tell you. I see a nosy woman who doesn't know when to quit, a woman who pushes and prods and has to know every damn thing, even if it has nothing to do with her. A woman who should leave well enough alone.'

She paled, her blue eyes stark orbs in her face, but he couldn't let a flash of pity for her stop what he had to do. In a way, this hadn't come at the best time. He hadn't meant to say half of that, the words spilling out in anger, but it was too late. The damage was done and she stared at him like he was some kind of monster.

He could've bundled her into his arms and apologised. He could've told her the truth about what being a

Burrell meant: he was stubborn, proud and ambitious, three traits that didn't bode well for family life, traits that could ultimately kill emotion, and he had them in spades.

He'd been too stubborn to acknowledge his true dream years earlier when he could've saved himself years of grinding away in a career that was slowly killing him.

He'd been too proud to accept his father's help when he'd finally made the break.

And his relentless ambition to get to the top of his profession and stay there was what drove him every day, what woke his muse up in the morning and what would ultimately drive away any person stupid enough to get close to him.

At the first glimpse of tears in her eyes, he took a step back, ready to end this conversation here and now.

'I don't appreciate you interfering in my life, so butt out.'

Pain warred with pity and the pain won out, her stare shimmering with tears and acting like a sucker punch to his gut.

She felt sorry for him for being such a heartless bastard. And he'd hurt her more than he'd ever wanted to.

'I guess that's been the problem all along. You don't appreciate me much, period.'

She pushed past him and ran for the flat, her sandals clattering against the floorboards in loud, staccato sounds so like the hammer driving inch-long nails into his heart.

CHAPTER THIRTEEN

Wally liked being organised. A place for everything and everything in its place. However, today his burrow seemed too tidy, too stark. He liked it when Prue the Platypus or Eddy the Echidna dropped by for a cup of billy tea or a bit of bush tucker. However, today he particularly wanted to see one visitor, but Kaz had vanished. She'd been so mad at him last night. He'd thought about digging all the way to China, but he couldn't even summon up the energy to do that.
Bo Bradford's blog, Wednesday.

SEEING the note propped up against his computer didn't surprise Bo in the least as he entered the office, rubbing a hand over his gritty eyes. He hadn't slept all night, his head filled with the lousy way he'd treated Tahnee.

She hadn't deserved his wrath and no matter how much he wanted to avoid the personal twist their relationship had taken, he shouldn't have driven her away like that.

They were a good team, dynamic business partners, and he'd probably ruined what little chance he had of patching their working relationship because of a childish bout of temper.

Snatching the note, he unfolded it, her bold, flowing script so indicative of the bold vitality of the woman who'd penned it.

> Bo,
> I'll be working from my sister's apartment till the end of the week and the conclusion of our business arrangement. You can email me the last two Wally scenes at the email address on my résumé. I'll finish the remaining sketches and get them back to you. Wages due can be forwarded to my home address.
> Best of luck with your writing,
> Tahnee

He crumpled the note in his fist, hating the finality of her words, hating the way his heart lurched.

He'd botched it.

Well and truly stuffed up the greatest opportunity to land in his lap ever. For a guy who had a way with words, he sure hadn't found the right ones to use with Tahnee.

That's when it hit him.

Fair and square, right between the eyes, a knockout punch to his reeling head and he staggered back and collapsed in his chair like a prize-fighter on the ropes for the last time.

Her note was all business—plain speaking and to the point, as Tahnee had always been with him, yet, when he'd referred to the greatest opportunity a second ago, business had been furthest from his mind.

He'd been thinking about losing her, every delicious, sassy, outspoken inch of her, and it left him struggling for air.

But if the soul-deep emptiness spreading through him wasn't about business, that meant…

He groaned, shaking his head, hoping the rapid movement might clear it. It didn't work and he had a sneaking suspicion nothing would till he admitted the truth.

He loved her.

The stupidest, dumbest move a guy like him could make, a guy who valued his independence above all else, a guy who didn't have the foggiest idea how to be part of a couple, a guy who was too wrapped up in his fantasy world, creating fictional characters, to take the risk of entering the real world ever again.

He couldn't love her.

He'd never experienced the much-touted emotion with a woman, let alone knew what it was. How could a guy who'd never known love identify it?

Closing his eyes, he dredged up every memory he could that he equated with his version of love: his first Christmas, age four, when his dad had taken a whole day off work to spend with the family.

The first time he'd ridden a horse, the first time his folks had come to watch him play footy, his first kiss at age ten with a much older twelve-year-old and the many times he'd seen genuine affection in his dad's eyes around the offices at Burrell Finance.

His only experience with love had been the familial kind, where your parents or siblings accepted you for who you were regardless of whether you're a major pain in the ass or not. As for women…he knew jack.

Not surprisingly, Kay didn't feature in his warm and fuzzy memories. She'd been an accessory to his life back then, the type of girlfriend who wanted to get ahead rather than get serious. Love hadn't entered the equation and, sadly, he hadn't missed it at the time.

Unlike now, when the thought of never seeing Tahnee again, of not hearing her contagious laugh, of not seeing her sleepy half smile first thing in the morning, of never holding her or tasting her or making love to her ever again acted like a kick in the guts, leaving him sick and sorry and gasping for air.

He'd already paid the ultimate price in seeing a lot less of his family while following his dream. What if hiding himself away from the world cost him the woman he loved, too?

He had to do something before it was too late.

Tahnee opened the door to Kristen's apartment, stepped into it and sagged with relief.

She'd done it.

Walking away from Bo should've been the hardest thing in the world, but he'd made it easy for her last night.

She should be thanking him.

Instead, she dropped her bags at the door, slammed it shut and headed for the sofa, curling onto her side while battling tears. Wriggling, she tried to get comfortable, but her sister's trendy chrome-legged, leather combo was built for style, not comfort. Unlike Bo's, where she'd happily curled up every day, working with a burst of creativity she'd never experienced before.

'Stop it,' she said, grabbing a cushion and hugging it tight, as much a defence against the crazy person she'd become for chastising herself out loud as any other reason.

She'd told herself on the way over here she wouldn't do this. She wouldn't think about him, wouldn't dwell on the last ten days or dredge up the endless store of memories of the time they'd spent together.

She had a job to do. She was a professional and she always delivered her work on time. She had a reputation as a businesswoman and one of the best at that. No way would she let a teensy-weensy broken heart stand in her way.

She promptly burst into tears.

Making angry swipes at the useless tears trickling down her cheeks, she got up, flung the cushion away and grabbed her bag. She needed a distraction and right now, answering the gazillion text messages Nina had left her seemed a good idea.

Her best friend would be frantic by now, but she'd been so caught up in the drama of the last few days she hadn't been able to text Nina, let alone respond to her three voice messages. Besides, the last time they'd spoken had been over coffee, she'd envisaged a rosy future and Nina had been one hundred per cent supportive as usual.

Maybe she should ignore Nina's messages?

Yeah, right.

Tahnee knew if she didn't respond soon, Nina would be more than likely to arrive on Bo's doorstep.

Not a good idea, considering she'd moved out and had now taken up residence in her jet-setting sister's apartment. Ironic, considering her other sister Carissa had holed up here when her now-husband Brody hadn't realised they had a future.

Not that she was expecting similar miracles from Bo. He had as much chance of showing up on her doorstep with a marriage proposal as she did of climbing the Harbour Bridge—an impossibility, considering her fear of heights.

She flipped open the phone, contemplating ringing for all of two seconds before realising it was a dumb idea. Nina would hear her choked voice and blocked nose, Tahnee would start bawling again and having her overzealous friend drive down here to ply her with tissues and advice was not what she needed right now.

She needed time to recover, time to finish her work and time to get herself together before she went home.

Aware she had to tell Nina something, she stabbed at the tiny alphabet buttons on her phone, composing a message totally at odds with her churned-up, blubbering self.

HEY N.,
SORRY I'VE BEEN SILENT.
BUSY WITH WORK.
TELL ALL WHEN I C U.
T. xx

Hitting the send button, she waited for the almost instant response she expected from her curious friend. The phone beeped a second later and she managed a rueful smile. Nina must've had the phone glued to her side to have answered that quickly.

BAD GIRL.
I WAS WORRIED.
U SURE U'R OK?
WHEN WILL I C U?
N. xox

Sooner than Nina thought, because her trial at the dream job had withered and died along with her hopes for a future with the dream man.

Though maybe she'd stay here a while longer, a week or two after she'd handed in the final sketches. No use rushing back to Stockton where Nina would smother her in her personal brand of remedies for the broken-hearted which usually consisted of copious amounts of chocolate, Kahlúa and romance novels to try and prove love really did conquer all.

She'd laughed when Nina had forced her pick-me-up packs on the lovelorn of Stockton before, but now that she would be the recipient, it wasn't so funny any more, and part of the reason why she'd headed for the anonymity of Kristen's apartment rather than heading home.

Anonymity...great, maybe she'd caught the emotionless-hermit disease from Bo?

She had to reassure Nina once and for all, then she could get down to the serious business of wallowing in peace.

> I'M OK.
> C U SOON.
> I'LL CALL.
> T. xx

Thankfully, Nina got the underlying message and her mobile remained silent, so she tossed it back in her bag, lay back on the sofa and closed her eyes, determined not to waste one more tear on a guy who didn't deserve them.

Now, if she could only erase her memory banks of the last week and a half, the too-few days when she'd had the time of her life, she'd be happy.

Bo had wasted an hour trying to come up with a suitable response to Tahnee's note, something that wouldn't sound too strong, too weak or too desperate. A hard task in itself, considering he'd never been so desperate to see anyone, to have a chance to explain, but the words wouldn't flow and, for the umpteenth time over the last few days, he stared at a blank screen.

He hated having to email her such an important

message when he'd much rather talk to her face to face, though she hadn't left him much choice. He seemed to have lost her mobile number, and unfortunately her résumé only had a home phone number, but she'd gone to her sister's.

He remembered her mentioning she had a sister working overseas who kept an apartment in Sydney, but, for the life of him, he couldn't remember where. Not that it would do him much good. She'd probably slam the door in his face if he had the audacity to show up unannounced after the way he'd last spoken to her.

Damn, he'd treated her badly.

He'd been so wrapped up in himself as usual, putting his needs first, ramming home his point of view to assert the upper hand.

But he wasn't in the financial world any more and he didn't have to prove anything to anybody, particularly not to a woman who had laid her heart on the line for him and which he'd trampled without a second thought.

He'd spent too long holed up in this place, trying to forge a career and follow his dream, which had taken precedence over everything else, including having a life.

He needed to wake up and smell the bush flowers alongside his good mate Wally.

He needed to get a life.

Suddenly propelled into action, he typed a quick, honest email to Tahnee before he had time to mull over it.

HEY TAHNEE,
SORRY FOR THE WAY THINGS ENDED.

I MUCKED UP TOTALLY.
WOULD LIKE A CHANCE TO EXPLAIN.
HOW ABOUT JOINING KAZ, PRUE, EDDY AND WALLY AT MY PLACE FOR A POW-WOW? OR THE GANG CAN COME TO YOU, WHICHEVER'S EASIEST?
HOPE TO HEAR FROM YOU SOON,
BO

Okay, so it wasn't some of his best work, but he hoped the humour would give him a shot at breaking through her defences, which she had every right to erect after the way he'd treated her.

Pushing her away had been a natural reaction born of years of hibernation. But maybe it was time to change the rules, just like she had. Shake them up a little, see what happened.

Clicking on the Send button, he waited at the computer for the next ten minutes, desperate to hear an answering beep that said he had mail. The silence was deafening and he clicked on the Internet icon, idly scanning the latest Amazon rankings with little interest.

Who cared about sales when he'd potentially ruined the best thing to have ever happened to him?

What seemed like an eternity later, his computer beeped, signalling he had mail, and his hand shook as he opened his inbox to see if Tahnee had responded.

Holding his breath, he punched the air when he saw an email from her. She'd responded. Yes.

YOU DID MUCK UP.

YOU MADE A RIGHT WALLY OF YOURSELF!

WILLING TO SEE YOU GROVEL ON FRIDAY ONCE FINAL SCENES COMPLETED.

I'LL DROP THEM IN AT YOUR PLACE, SIX O'CLOCK.

BUT DON'T EXPECT MIRACLES.

TAHNEE

He reread her email five times, trying to decipher it.

Was she still mad as hell or thawing?

She'd attempted humour with the Wally comment, but what did she mean by miracles? Was she referring to her work on the final part of the book or forgiving him for acting like a jerk?

This was exactly why he didn't do emotions. They confused the hell out of him.

After sending a brief 'great, see you then' response, he swung out of his chair and headed for the door. He needed to clear his clogged head and a swim should do the trick, followed by a nice long session with a psychotherapist to help him figure out how on earth he was going to convince the woman he loved to take a chance on a guy like him.

CHAPTER FOURTEEN

Wally spent all day fixing up the new hole he'd dug. Kaz was coming for a visit. He hadn't seen her in ages and he'd missed her. If he was really, really nice to her, maybe she'd want to stick around. He'd like that. His new digs were no fun without her. What would convince her to stay? He'd thought long and hard before coming up with a brilliant idea. Kaz loved chocolate topping. Maybe if he bought her a crateful...
Bo Bradford's blog, Friday.

As TAHNEE buzzed the intercom at Bo's front gate, she closed her eyes and leant back against the headrest.

She had to be nuts. Crazy, mad, completely certifiable to be doing this.

What was she thinking?

As the gates swung open, she knew the answer.

She wasn't thinking.

Ever since she'd entered these gates two weeks ago

her brain had gone into hibernation and no amount of coaxing could bring her common sense out.

She should've deleted Bo's email the moment it hit her inbox.

She should've ignored it or practised rude replies without sending them before deleting it.

She should've told him to stick it.

Instead, here she was, dolled up in her favourite white denim hipsters, tight orange T-shirt and enough mascara and lip gloss to give her a confidence boost, ready to march into enemy territory, pretend she didn't give a damn and steel herself against whatever pitiful excuses he might give for his behaviour, before heading back to Stockton a basket case.

Pulling up at the front door, she ignored the strong wave of déjà vu, grabbed her bag with the final sketches and headed for the house. Ringing the bell, she waited, hating the feeling of being a visitor when she'd learned to treat this place like her own.

Strange, considering she never took to houses quickly. She had her dream home in mind and nowhere else had ever lived up to it, yet Bo's house had drawn her in, made her feel welcome and secure, a surprise in itself. She had never felt secure, no matter how successful or how much money or how many friends she had. It just never seemed enough, yet she'd felt secure here, in this house, in this guy's arms.

The guy who'd just opened the door and smiled at her as if she were the best present he'd ever received.

'I brought your sketches.'

Okay, so it sucked as an opening line, but it was all she could manage at the moment. Besides, witty repartee wasn't her forte when her mind zeroed straight to the bedroom, remembering how good Bo looked, particularly without the jeans and polo he was wearing.

'Great, come on in.'

She brushed past him, head held high, senses reeling as she caught the familiar smell of his aftershave, the subtle blend of spice and oak imprinted on her receptors for ever.

Clamping down on the overwhelming desire to drop the sketches at the door and either run, or jump him, she marched towards the kitchen before belatedly realising it probably wasn't the best place to meet.

Too much had happened in that kitchen: too many memories, too many opportunities to slip up and act on them.

Taking a steadying breath, she stepped into the kitchen, headed for the table and whipped out her sketches. The sooner they focused on business and she got out of here, clothes and dignity intact, the better.

'Can I get you anything?'

He propped himself against a bench top, wearing the same, sexy smile that had robbed her of every ounce of common sense she'd ever had and she bit back her instant response of 'you.'

She shook her head, pointing to the sketches.

'Your final two scenes were brilliant. Hope I've done them justice.'

He crossed the kitchen and stood next to her, invading her personal space, sending her body crazy.

She was supposed to be mad at this guy.

She was supposed to hate him for not loving her, for being so business-oriented, for seeing their only connection beyond today as a work 'arrangement.'

But the longer he stood there, radiating a potent heat that enticed her to lean towards him, she couldn't think of anything bar how much she wanted to sweep her work onto the floor and have her way with him on the table.

'These are great. You've excelled yourself.'

Ha, easy for him to say.

She'd been up all night, putting the finishing touches to the sketches, determined to show him how professional she could be when all she wanted to do was smash the pictures over his obtuse head.

'Good. Now that's finished, I'll be leaving—'

'What did you think of the ending?'

She finally looked up, meeting his gaze for the first time, hating the treacherous lurch of her heart as dazzling green connected with confused blue.

'The ending was cute, like all your books.'

His gaze never wavered, boring into her as if trying to convey some hidden message she couldn't comprehend.

'Yeah, but did you like how Wally and Kaz finally got their act together?'

Suddenly, a light bulb went off in her head.

He couldn't be serious.

Surely he wasn't implying he was Wally and she

was Kaz? But that would mean he wanted a happy ending for them... As if.

'The ending was good, but personally I thought Wally was too much of a dufus for a smart kangaroo like Kaz. She should've kicked him to the watering hole and back for acting how he did for so long.'

His face fell and she almost laughed out loud.

This was too easy.

'Don't you think Wally deserved brownie points for coming to his senses before it was too late?'

She shook her head.

'Nah...Kaz let him off too easy. He was an emotionally repressed, uptight waddler and she had more spunk in her tail than he did in his whole neurotic body. She should never have given him a second chance. He didn't deserve it.'

Bo stared at her, horror mingling with regret in his eyes, and she couldn't contain the laughter bubbling up any longer.

He frowned as she doubled over. 'What's so funny?'

'You are,' she gasped, holding her sides and laughing harder. 'Wally!'

His frown lingered for a second longer before fading away, the corners of his mouth twitching till he joined in her uncontrollable laughter. 'I'm that transparent?'

'You're a pane of glass,' she said, her chuckles petering out as she straightened, wishing they could stay like this for ever. Close, happy, sharing a funny moment in a cosy room that held great memories.

But this wasn't a fantasy and memories had a way of

fading when not sustained, a bit like their relationship, which was over before it had even started thanks to him.

'So there's no chance of a happy ending for us?'

She stared him down, hating the flicker of hope leaping to life in her heart. 'Sorry, but as I've already told you, I can't accept your offer to work with you.'

His eyes widened in surprise. 'I'm not talking about work.'

'Oh.'

Then what the heck was he on about? He couldn't be talking about…

'I'm talking about us and the possibility you want to throw every rule out the window and start over.'

Her jaw dropped and she quickly snapped it shut, just in case he took it as an invitation. Not that she was averse to kissing him, but right now she needed to make sure she wasn't delusional and had actually heard correctly.

'Before you say anything, I need to apologise for the way I reacted after you found out my true identity. You were only being curious and I acted like a jerk. I'm sorry.'

'Apology accepted.'

Now, could they get back to the good stuff? The part where he wanted to start over.

'I owe you an explanation.'

'You owe me nothing.' She couldn't give a flying hoot about his identity when there were larger matters at stake, namely her heart. 'Apart from two weeks' wages, that is.'

A rueful smile crossed his face. 'After putting up

with my boorish behaviour, you deserve a year's worth. But I do want to explain some stuff to you.'

Okay, so he'd said the right thing and sucked her in. She couldn't walk away from a good mystery unravelling any more than she could walk away from him.

'Go ahead,' she said, hoping she hadn't just given him licence to explain away his behaviour and kill her hopes for their future once and for all.

'Being a Burrell is great. Too great. People have always bowed and scraped and opened doors just because of who I am and the family I was lucky enough to be born into. When I wanted to write, I needed to prove something to myself, that I could succeed in something without having anyone give me a helping hand along the way because I was Bo Burrell. So I swore my dad and Brennan to secrecy, bought this place with the money I'd made through financing and dropped out of society. I didn't want any favours, even from my dad, and I wanted to make it on my own. I love writing, but I reckoned I chose this profession for a reason, for the solitude and lack of people contact, which I'd had a gutful of anyway. It felt so damn good to walk away from it all and thankfully my family understood. Now I hope you can.'

He reached towards her, taking hold of her hand; she didn't have the heart to tug it away.

Not that she minded the sizzle of electricity from his touch or the warmth it evoked, but she couldn't give in this easily.

What if this was a ploy to suck her back in to work

for him? She didn't think he could be that low, but then again she didn't have a lot of experience with the weaselly gender.

'Being an author is everything I dreamed of, but I've paid a price. I can't spend time with my family in public any more because people will hound them for the truth behind my 'disappearance.' I can't go sailing with my dad and Brennan like I used to, I can't hang out or drop by the office for a chat. It's been tough, but I've handled it by shutting myself away and focusing on the good side of being a recluse. Then you came along, and you encapsulated everything I'm afraid of. You're vivacious and bubbly and love people. You thrive in the company of others—I saw it first-hand at the awards night. You shine and dazzle, whereas I've been there, done that, never want to return. And worse, you bring out that side of me. You make me want to have fun and play and live for the moment, a scary proposition for a hermit like me. But it's time I stopped hiding away, time to join the real world, with you by my side hopefully.'

He squeezed her hand, his eyes imploring her to understand, to forgive, and the ice around her heart thawed a tad.

'Pretty big turnaround. What brought it on?'

She should be doing cartwheels since he'd opened up and, even better, wanted her in his life other than as a colleague. But she couldn't shake the feeling there was more, that there was some piece of this puzzle that didn't fit.

He shrugged, a sheepish expression on his face.

'We're a great team, not just in the office. Guess it took me a while to figure it out.'

And just like that, the final, odd-shaped piece slid into place, completing the picture and leaving her more devastated than before.

Sex. He was talking about the amazing sex they'd had.

He missed it and wanted them to get back into the swing of things.

How could she have been so stupid? Again!

He hadn't mentioned a relationship or love or any of the words she'd wanted to hear and, for a short time there, had thought he was hinting at.

Uh-uh. He wasn't getting any and he wanted it back.

So what did he think, she'd pop in for a quickie whenever she was in Sydney?

Fury surged through her body and she yanked her hand out of his, fumbling for her bag and knocking it to the floor in her haste.

Cursing, she bent to retrieve the contents of her bag now scattered across the floor and he helped her, handing her a pen, chewing gum, and then a tampon. She blushed and snatched it out of his hand.

'Hey, I know this is a bit of a surprise but I thought you might want to talk about it, see where we go from here, maybe give it another go?'

'I just bet you did,' she snapped, standing and slinging her bag over her shoulder, wishing she'd worn flats rather than heels so she could make a run for the door. 'Sorry, I'm not in the mood any more.'

Confusion clouded his eyes and she snorted in disgust. 'Cut the act. Or do you want me to spell it out for you?'

Hugging her bag to her chest like a shield, she said, 'Fine, I'll spell it out for you. I'm not interested. Got that?'

He stepped back as if she'd physically struck him, pain slashing his face.

'Loud and clear,' he said, staring at her like she'd morphed into a two-headed monster. 'I won't bother you again.'

'Good.'

She willed her feet to move, but for some reason they didn't respond as she stared at him like an onlooker at a car accident, hating the devastation, but unable to look away.

For a guy who'd received a knock back, he looked pretty cut up about it. Worse, he looked like someone had died. Good, now he knew what she felt like inside as her heart shrivelled up for the last time.

'It's only sex. Don't look so worried, a guy like you will have no trouble finding a replacement for me.'

His head snapped up as he took a step towards her.

'What did you just say?'

Rolling her eyes, she wondered if he was doing this whole obtuse act on purpose as a way to gain sympathy.

'You heard me. I guess a city boy like you thought a country girl like me might enjoy a bit of nooky every time she came into town, but trust me, you'd be better off finding someone nearer to home, someone to call on whenever you get the urge.'

Shaking his head, he grabbed her arms, his fingers biting into her.

'I can't believe you just said that.' The pain in his eyes struck anew. 'I can't believe you think I'm like that.'

A niggle of doubt wormed its way into her head.

What if she was wrong?

What if she'd jumped to conclusions to explain away her own feelings of inadequacy?

'Well, what am I supposed to think? You talk about picking up where we left off, how we're a good team out of the office, as well as in it. The way I see it, the only other teamwork we did out of office hours involved sex, so tell me, what am I supposed to think?'

Pain leached from his steady stare, only to be replaced by sadness.

'You could think I'm the kind of guy who wouldn't treat you like that. You could think I'm interested in more than your body. You could even think I'm hinting at a relationship, but hey, maybe I've been holed up in this house so long I'm talking in riddles and expecting you to understand.'

Her heart tripped and flipped and turned on itself. 'Did you just say relationship?'

Nah…he couldn't have. Maybe guys used relationship these days as a euphemism for affair or fling or whatever it was they called no-strings-attached sex.

Releasing her arms, he captured her face between his hands, heat blazing from his eyes and warming her better than the Bondi sun on a hot summer's day.

'I can see I'm going to have to spell this out for you.'

Brushing her cheeks with his thumbs, trailing his fingertips along her jaw, he said, 'I love you. I want a relationship with you. Hell, I want to marry you and watch you stub your toes and give yourself concussions and do all the other crazy things you do because I'm crazy about you. There, is that clear enough for you?'

Pure, indescribable joy filled her and she lunged at him, plastering her lips to his, kissing him till she couldn't breathe.

'I take it you like the idea?'

She laughed and hugged him tighter.

'For an author, you have a lousy way with words. Why didn't you say all that stuff at the start?'

His sexy grin set her pulse racing again. 'And make it easy for you? Where's the fun in that?'

She swatted him, wrapping her arms around his waist, secure in his embrace, knowing there was no place else she'd rather be.

'You do know I love you, too, right?'

'Right.'

'And I want to make babies with you?'

His grin turned goofy. 'Riiight.'

'And I've got my heart set on the whole white-picket fence, mud-brick cottage dream in my home town?'

'How about we spend some time there, some time here?'

She pretended to think for a moment, capitulating when he tickled her ribs.

'Fine. And you know there'll be a whole new set of ground rules?'

He growled and nuzzled her neck, kissing his way up to her mouth where she welcomed his hot, open-mouth kiss, instant heat turning her body to liquid fire.

'No more rules,' he murmured against the side of her mouth, trailing his lips along her cheek to her earlobe where he nibbled and nipped till she squealed.

Placing her hands on his chest, she bunched his T-shirt in her fingers. 'Hey! Don't you know the best bit about rules?'

A wary expression crossed his face. 'What?'

'They're made to be broken.'

She laughed as he hauled her into his arms and proceeded to show her exactly how.

EPILOGUE

Wally liked having two homes. He liked the trips between burrows, he liked having friends at both watering holes, but best of all he liked having Kaz around. She made him laugh, she made him the best bush-tucker dinners, but most of all she made him feel like the luckiest wombat in the whole of Australia. Kaz was the coolest.
Bo Bradford's blog, three months later.

'HOW'S THAT final sketch coming along?'

Tahnee glanced up from her sketchpad and glared at Bo, smiling at her from behind his laptop.

'Slave-driver.'

He held up his hands in protest.

'Hey, I wasn't the one who impressed the bosses so much at the awards night they offered us a three-book contract with killer deadlines.'

'Yeah, but you could've warned me I'd be constantly distracted and find it difficult to work.'

Her gaze roved over him, from his upper body

clearly delineated in pale blue cotton to his bare legs poking out from camel-coloured shorts under the desk, her pulse humming in anticipation of another 'distraction.'

Grinning, he clasped his hands and stretched overhead. 'You find me distracting, huh?'

'I find you irresistible.'

She threw her sketchpad down and crossed to the desk, plopping into his lap and wrapping her arms around his neck. 'And if we keep doing this, we're never going to make deadline.'

His hands skimming her back, he dipped his head for a quick kiss, murmuring against the side of her mouth, 'I do my best work under pressure. How about you?'

'I can't think when you're doing that,' she said, making a soft mewling sound of pleasure as he slipped his hands under her top and his fingertips danced across her skin.

'That's the whole point.'

He kissed her, the type of drugging, seductive fusion of lips that left her breathless and hot and turned on, craving his touch like she'd never get enough.

Sighing with regret, she broke the kiss.

'You know I have to finish that last sketch right now, don't you?'

He nodded, an impish gleam in his sparkling eyes.

'Yeah, I know. Just think how much fun we're going to have celebrating later. I have a crateful of chocolate topping waiting for us.'

'Ooh, you're a bad man.'

'And you love me for it. Particularly my creative

side, which comes up with all the new, inventive ways to use it.'

Knowing she'd go into complete meltdown any second now, she brushed her lips across his.

'Hold that thought.'

Wishing she didn't have to do this, she reluctantly disengaged from his arms and padded back to the sofa, his soft chuckles following her.

Easy for him to laugh. He hadn't turned into a raving nymphomaniac, the type of woman who wanted sex all the time when the man of her dreams so much as glanced her way.

Dropping down on the sofa, she picked up her sketchpad and held it up, determined not to look at him. No easy feat considering she couldn't keep her hands or her eyes off him these days.

The last few months had been a dream come true: working together, playing together, more playing together.

She hadn't bought the mud-brick cottage, with negotiations taking longer than expected, but it didn't bother her. Being with Bo, surrounded by his love on a daily basis, she'd finally realised that security wasn't about bricks and mortar or having a nest egg the size of an island. The unconditional, unswerving love of one guy had done more for her insecurities than any house could've ever done.

'Sorry to interrupt, but there's an email here from Nina, sent high priority, her third one of the day. What do you want me to do?'

She peeped over her pad for a second, like staring at

an eclipse. Any longer and she'd get burned for sure. At least, her body would burn up and she'd be forced to take off her clothes and they'd be right back to where they'd started—possibly missing a deadline for the first time because they couldn't keep their hands off each other.

'You know she thinks our lives run parallel to Wally and Kaz?'

'Yeah.'

'And she's glued to your blog for daily updates?'

'Yeah.'

'Well, she's been giving me a hard time lately about wedding stuff. Why don't we give our matron of honour a little something to stew over?'

Bo's eyes lit up. He had a great rapport with Nina and loved dishing it out as much as he took it from her, and it looked like he was up for a bit of teasing just as she anticipated.

'Great idea. Leave it with me.'

Sending him a wink, she concentrated on putting the final touches on Wally and Kaz's outback party, complete with bush band and gum-tree marquee. After ten minutes' hard slog, where she refused to think of her sexy fiancé, let alone look at him, she finally threw down her charcoal, leapt to her feet and practically ran across the room.

'All finished.'

He smiled and opened his arms to her. 'Funny, I'm just getting started.'

His sizzling look scorched her from the inside out and she took the best seat in the house: his lap.

'Me, too, but I want to see what you sent Nina first.'

Chuckling, he swung her around to face the laptop, his arms circled snugly around her waist.

'Take a look.'

With a click of the mouse, Bo's blog came up, with Wally, Kaz, Prue and co. doing happy dances around the borders of the screen.

Tahnee scanned the page for the latest update, her eyes widening with delight when she spotted it.

WALLY WOULD LIKE WENDY THE WALLABY TO STOP NOSING AROUND HIS BURROW. KAZ IS GETTING JUMPY, WHAT WITH A POSSIBLE JOEY JOINING THE GANG. WALLY KNOWS WENDY IS KAZ'S BEST FRIEND, BUT MAYBE SHE SHOULD HOP TO IT FOR NOW AND NOSE AROUND SOMEWHERE ELSE?

She laughed and swung to face him. 'You didn't really post that on your blog, did you? You can't lie like that.'

He shook his head, joining in her laughter.

'No. That's just the template I sent to Nina.'

'You've done it now!'

His green eyes darkened as he traced a finger ever so slowly down her cheek. 'Actually, not yet. But I'm about to.'

Desire pooled deep within as she brushed a kiss across his lips. 'Rule number one: must say "I love you" to future wife before making incredible love to her.'

'I love you,' he murmured, tracing her lips in the barest of kisses. 'What's rule number two?'

'Rule number two: must draw out foreplay as long as possible to drive future wife mad with lust for her sexy future husband.'

'How's this for a start?'

A familiar shiver of awareness rippled through her body as his hands traced lazy circles in the middle of her back, moving with slow, exquisite precision downwards, lower and lower till he touched her butt and settled her firmly over his bulging erection.

'And how about this?'

His kiss was hot and urgent, his tongue delving into her mouth, begging her to join him in the agonisingly sweet build-up to the ultimate pleasure he created every time he got her naked and panting with need for him.

'Wow,' she murmured when his lips left hers, searing a path across her cheek to the sensitive hollow below her ear.

'What's rule number three?' he whispered a second before nipping her with a gentle bite that had her arching up in desperate need to have more of that special treatment all over her body.

'Rules-schmules,' she said, snuggling deeper into his arms, welcoming his caresses, secure in the knowledge she'd finally come home.

0307/06

MILLS & BOON

Modern
romance™
Extra

Two longer and more passionate stories every month

GETTING DOWN TO BUSINESS
by Ally Blake

If prim Abbey Parish wants to get sexy playboy and tycoon Flynn Granger on board with her business, she's going to have to loosen up a little… Flynn's impressed with Abbey's ideas, but if he could just get beneath her suited-and-booted persona, he's certain he'll find a wild and sensual woman underneath. Then getting down to business with Abbey would get a whole load more interesting!

BEDDED BY A BAD BOY by Heidi Rice

Monroe Latimer is a drop-dead gorgeous bad boy who doesn't do commitment. One look at Monroe and feisty English girl Jessie Connor knows he's about as Mr Wrong as a guy can get, but there's one big problem. He's sexy as hell, he fires her blood like no other man ever has and his killer blue gaze is focused right on her. His look says he'll bed her – but never wed her… Is Jessie the one who can tame the untameable?

On sale 6th April 2007

Available at WHSmith, Tesco, ASDA, and all good bookshops
www.millsandboon.co.uk

Modern
romance

THE MARRIAGE POSSESSION by Helen Bianchin
Lisane Deveraux is a successful lawyer by day and Zac Winstone's passionate mistress by night. But a surprise pregnancy changes everything and Zac proposes. Lisane prepares herself for a life as Zac's trophy wife in public and his mistress in private... His heart will never be part of the deal...

THE SHEIKH'S UNWILLING WIFE
by Sharon Kendrick
Five years ago Alexa walked out on her marriage, taking with her a precious secret. Giovanni is the son of a powerful desert ruler and he's determined that Alexa should resume her position as his wife. But how will he react when he discovers he has a son...?

THE ITALIAN'S INEXPERIENCED MISTRESS
by Lynne Graham
When Angelo set out to get revenge, innocent Gwenna Hamilton reluctantly accepted the Italian tycoon's offer to pay for her father's freedom with her body. Gwenna thought Angelo would tire of her and her inexperience quickly. But he wanted more than just one night...

THE SICILIAN'S VIRGIN BRIDE by Sarah Morgan
All billionaire Rocco Castellani had wished for was a biddable wife – instead Francesca had gone before the first dance at their wedding! But Rocco has tracked her down... He was cheated out of his wedding night – and nothing is going to stop him claiming his virgin bride...

On sale 6th April 2007

Available at WHSmith, Tesco, ASDA, and all good bookshops

www.millsandboon.co.uk

MILLS & BOON

0307/01b

Modern
romance™

THE RICH MAN'S BRIDE by Catherine George
Ever since Anna Morton was snubbed by wealthy Ryder Wyndham she's kept her distance from the man she once worshipped. Then Anna is forced to live with Ryder, and tension turns to temptation... Anna has no plans to settle down – but Ryder is determined that she will be his lady-of-the-manor bride!

WIFE BY CONTRACT, MISTRESS BY DEMAND by Carole Mortimer
Gabriella Benito fell for her wealthy stepbrother Rufus Gresham the day she set eyes on him. But Rufus believed she was a gold digger... Then they are obliged to marry to secure their inheritances. At the wedding, Rufus kisses Gabriella passionately – is he using their marriage as an excuse to get her in his bed...?

WIFE BY APPROVAL by Lee Wilkinson
Richard Anders is heir to the sumptuous Castle Anders and needs gorgeous Valentina to secure his birthright. Valentina is swept off her feet by this handsome gentleman. Soon she's given him her innocence in the bedroom, she's given him her word at the altar, but when she learns the truth will she give Richard her heart?

THE SHEIKH'S RANSOMED BRIDE by Annie West
Kidnapped by rebels, Belle Winters is rescued by Rafiq al Akhtar, Sovereign Prince of the desert kingdom of Q'aroum. Whisked away to his exotic palace, she learns that Rafiq expects her to show her gratitude by marrying him! Rafiq intends her to carry out her royal duties both in public – and in private...

On sale 6th April 2007

Available at WHSmith, Tesco, ASDA, and all good bookshops
www.millsandboon.co.uk

0307/05a

MILLS & BOON

In April 2007 Mills & Boon present two classic collections, each featuring three wonderful romances by three of our bestselling authors…

Mediterranean Weddings

Featuring
A Mediterranean Marriage by Lynne Graham
The Greek's Virgin Bride by Julia James
The Italian Prince's Proposal by Susan Stephens

On sale 6th April 2007

Available at WHSmith, Tesco, ASDA, and all good bookshops
www.millsandboon.co.uk

MILLS & BOON

0307/05b

Whose Baby?

Featuring
With This Baby... by Caroline Anderson
The Italian's Baby by Lucy Gordon
Assignment: Baby by Jessica Hart

Don't miss out on these superb stories!

On sale 6th April 2007

Available at WHSmith, Tesco, ASDA, and all good bookshops
www.millsandboon.co.uk

Blaze

ROOM SERVICE by Jill Shalvis
Do Not Disturb

TV producer Em Harris has to convince chef Jacob Hill to sign up to her new show. But when she sets foot in Hush, the sex-themed hotel where Jacob works, she develops an insatiable craving for the sinfully delicious chef…

WHY NOT TONIGHT? by Jacquie D'Alessandro
24 Hours: Blackout

When Adam Clayton fills in at his friend's photography studio, he never dreamed he'd be taking *boudoir* photos – of his old flame! Mallory is just recently single, but luckily for Adam, a blackout gives him a chance to make her forget anyone but him…

HER BODY OF WORK by Marie Donovan

Undercover agent Marco Flores had ended up working as a model. A nude model. He'd taken the job to protect his brother, but he soon discovered the perks. Like having his sculptress, sexy Rey Martinson, end up as uncovered as him…

BASIC TRAINING by Julie Miller

Marine captain Travis McCormick can't believe it when Tess Bartlett – his best friend and new physiotherapist – asks for basic training in sex. Tess has been working on her battle plan for years, and its time to put it to work. She'll heal him…if he makes her feel good!

On sale 6th April 2007

Available at WHSmith, Tesco, ASDA, and all good bookshops
www.millsandboon.co.uk

Office romance has never been this fun!

Boardroom Brides
by Raye Morgan

Three sassy secretaries are about to land the deal of a lifetime!

On sale 16th February 2007

Boardroom Bridegrooms
by Liz Fielding

It's a marriage takeover for these dynamic business tycoons – with power struggles in the boardroom and romantic tussles in the bedroom!

On sale 16th March 2007

Available at WHSmith, Tesco, ASDA and all good bookshops

www.millsandboon.co.uk

The weekly magazine you'll use every day!

Woman's Weekly

Why not take out a subscription for your Woman's Weekly? Call 0845 676 7778 quoting 20A, or visit www.ipcsubs.co.uk/iwka

On sale every Wednesday

- Cookery
- Health
- Fiction
- Fashion
- Home
- Beauty
- Gardening
- Real-life stories, and much, much more